**also by ash lingam**

cowboys and pirates

cowboys and pirates

Ash Lingam

WISE WOLF
BOOKS

WISE WOLF BOOKS
An Imprint of Wolfpack Publishing
wisewolfbooks.com
1707 E. Diana Street
Tampa, FL 33610

Paperback ISBN 978-1-965596-52-4
eBook ISBN 978-1-965596-51-7

I wrote this book for my grandchildren, Kai, Ziggy, and Kalani. I hope when they grow up, they will read Grandpa's book about Cowboys & Pirates.

"Heaven, you fool. Did you ever hear of any pirates going thither? Give me hell; it's a merrier place."

—Pirate Capt. Thomas Sutton

cowboys and pirates

hurricane no. 7

In the Future—Off the coast of South America

THE THREE-MASTED schooner cut through the storm swells at over eight knots while the sails billowed and tugged against the rigging. The ship's bow sliced through the water with the grace of a ballerina on the world's largest stage. White frothy bubbles emerged from the sea and washed over the wooden deck and out the scuppers. Fueled by summer's warm waters, the wind howled like a forlorn beast. The Caribbean slammed against the ship as it reached a crest and roared down the massive wave, yowling its descent into the trough. Great white turbulent breakers crashed against the quarterdeck where the giant pilot's wheel stood.

A simple black flag flapped at the top of the main-sail in the force-twelve gusts, but the captain kept the bow turned toward the churning sea and laughed like a madman. His cat-green eye flashed with delight as he challenged the hurricane boiling before him. A blood vessel, dark blue with stress, pulsated at his temple as he peered wildly with his one good eye into the mist.

The captain was nearing his mid-twenties and stood over six feet three inches tall. His massive chest and back pulled his coat tight around his body. He wore a length of beard that hung in dreadlocks nearly to his belt. He sported one black boot that came up to his knee, and his other leg was strapped to an articulately carved teak peg. His black leather eyepatch creased the skin on his face and marked his hairline.

Captain Horacio Hellsworth carried no less than six cap-and-ball, flintlock pistols, tucked into his shoulder harness, and a long sword hung from the left side of a wide leather belt. He also carried an assortment of knives. His matted beard was tied with blood-red ribbons, fluttering like small flags in the tropical winds that pounded the coasts of South America.

As the hurricane howled in Horacio's face, his long locks of hair flapped like small wet sails. But the captain's green eye did not lose its glee. Nick Risk, a Texan gunslinger, was the only man brave enough to accompany the pirate captain, daring the storm to take his life. Both men came from the dredges of their own respective hellish pasts and dispelled fear of any kind.

Unlike the other sailors on the vessel, the Texan-born American wore two large pistols in cross-draw holsters. A cowboy hat sat cocked on his head. Two more single-action .38 revolvers hung in a shoulder harness. Each time the large sailing vessel managed to reach the crest of the wave, the cowboy yelled out,

"Yippee-ki-yay!" while waving his pistol in the air and shooting off round after round. The barrel flashes illuminated the angry sky. He acted as though he was riding a wild stallion while he twirled a black bullwhip over his head with his other hand, making it crack like the thunder that roared among the dark clouds above.

The gunslinger's job was to protect the captain from his own crew, as well as his many enemies. The captain's actions often left the sailors disgruntled, especially on days when violent storms brewed. Nobody in their right mind would thumb their nose at Mother Nature.

The captain never treated his men with disregard, though, especially those eight orphans who had joined the ranks far before they secured and converted the *Black Widow* into a pirate warship.

Horacio Hellsworth's problem was an uncontrollable appetite for danger. He thought nothing of risking his own life and the lives of his sailors, too. The cowboy shared the captain's zest for peril. Both were orphaned at an early age and forced to mature well before their time.

Their strange relationship blossomed some years back when the captain was spying on ships, docked near Bridgetown in southwestern Barbados. He wanted to steal one of the vessels and sail away before anyone noticed.

Hellsworth had been drinking Cuban rum all day in a dark tavern on the edge of the harbor's red-light district when fate drew the cowboy and the pirate together. The two men joined in a partnership that would allow the seaman to complete his quest, secure the perfect vessel and begin an adventure that would span years and thousands of nautical miles.

As usual, Nick was at his side as bubbling whitecaps covered the ocean as far as the eye could see. High above, at the top of the main mast, sat a short, stocky sailor in the crow's nest. He was precariously perched at the ship's highest point while he kept an eye out for massive breakers and French, British, and Spanish warships—all serious threats in such turbulent waters.

Nick Risk, an ex-bounty hunter and gunfighter turned first mate, often was asked what the hell he was doing on a ship off the South American coast in the Caribbean Sea. He wondered, too, as the relentless storm battered the *Black Widow*.

During the hurricane, the cowboy shed his boots but not his ten-gallon-hat or repeater revolvers. Since Nick had left Galveston, his muscles resembled twisted mooring lines that rippled up and down his arms and back. The blonde-haired cowboy had piercing turquoise eyes and a mouthful of perfectly white teeth. He was the tallest man aboard the ship, towering over Captain Hellsworth, his massive frame stretching out to a full six feet seven.

His weapons were more advanced than any on board. He carried a brace of single-action, four-shot repeater revolvers he had acquired from a famous gunsmith and inventor. The pistols, part of a new era of weapon technology that would change the western frontier and beyond, gave him a considerable advantage in any skirmish.

The two Collier single-action wheel-guns were invented in 1820. They sported mother-of-pearl handles that glimmered whenever the sunlight penetrated the storm clouds. The prototype revolvers weren't sold on the American market yet. They gave Risk confidence because most sailors and adversaries were armed with flintlock, single-shot pistols or rifles. He also carried a sawed-off, double-barrel shotgun with a cut-down stock that fit perfectly in his massive paw.

In the back pocket of his britches, he hid a single-shot lady's pistol. It was small enough to hide in the palm of his hand but, at close range, could put a small chunk of lead into the eye of an opponent, where it would rattle around and wreak havoc on the brain. It was a secret he shared only with his best friend, Captain Hellsworth.

The *Black Widow* was one of the last half-dozen pirate ships sailing the Seven Seas in search of plunder. The glory days of the pirate lifestyle were over. Of course, Black Beard, and others like him, were feared in the 17th and 18th centuries. Now, the profession was approaching its end. Each of the die-hard crewmembers of the *Black Widow* could feel death's breath on their necks. They knew their days were numbered, but chose to make the best of it, good or bad,

As the skipper and his first mate stood at the helm of the *Black Widow*, both men's eyes shone with glee. Nothing pleased them more than the challenge of a battle—be it with Mother Nature or the ships of world's mightiest fleets. The vessels they sought to plunder were cargo ships that held valuable fortunes.

Some were warships, which provided a challenge the captain and first mate enjoyed. Warships also provided the possibility of acquiring more cannons for the *Black Widow*.

Known far and wide as "Hammer," Hellsworth always dressed in black, from his eyepatch to his boot. Only the ribbons tied to the ends of his braided beard provided contrast.

His tangled hair was so black it appeared deep blue and his eye turned dark as coal when he was angry. His leg was cut off just above the knee where the wooden peg began. Only the captain and the first mate knew that built into his pegleg was a cut-down flintlock musket. All he had to do was lift his stump, aim it at an adversary and pull the hidden trigger.

As a team, they were mentally and physically superior to the average individual. It's why they could capture and plunder ships successfully and manage their sometimes unruly crew. Any crewmember who thought he could challenge his superiors with sword or dagger, quickly was neutralized by the professional gunfighter.

The core of the crew, orphans and outcasts like the captain and first mate, were loyal beyond reproach to the masters of the *Black Widow*. The rest were sailors who had initially worked on other pirate vessels, so the leaders had to prove their worth along with their bravado.

To the newcomers, First Mate Risk was like a man from another planet, one they feared. He had served at the captain's side for thirty-eight months, ever since the *Black Widow* left Bridgetown.

As the three-masted ship crashed head-on with the Caribbean Sea, a lone sailor in the crow's nest spotted bounty on the boiling waters.

"Sails, Ho!" he called from the upper riggings of the ship.

"How many masts?" the captain cried back as he wrestled with the massive helm. "And how many cannons does she bear?"

"She's a three-masted cargo ship with sixteen guns plus two small cannons on the stern deck," the sailor shouted as he squinted through a spyglass.

"And her course?" Hammer demanded.

"Due north, Captain," the sailor called from aloft. "She's a cargo ship and flying the French flag. Should we strike our colors?"

The captain replied with a negative hand signal, turned to Risk and shouted, "There's no sense in running the black flag up yet. It would be impossible to board her in these storm swells. But we can stand off her starboard beam. She'll think we're just riding out the tail of the storm."

"Bring her around to due north in that case," the Texan said. Hammer spun the massive wheel twenty degrees to port and slowly began to pull alongside their target while keeping the *Black Widow* out of cannon range. Hellsworth didn't want the other ship to consider his actions aggressive.

"Have the men strike the French flag," the captain

ordered as Risk turned to Wishbone and relayed the instructions.

Of course, the *Black Widow* had an array of flags from many nations, as did most pirate ships. They hoisted the French flag to fool the poor souls on the vessel they followed. They also had English and American flags, along with Dutch, Argentinean, and Panamanian banners. They couldn't approach any vessel or a port without them, especially so in 1823 when pirate interception was waning.

Most seafaring vessels no longer feared being boarded by pirates. They were more concerned with their warring neighbors. The French hated the Spanish, and both despised the British, who were often at war with the Americans. So, every captain was wary of foreign ships.

Horacio steered the *Black Widow* into the mountainous seas the entire afternoon and on into the night, keeping the red port light just off their stern quarter. It gave the storm-weary crew of the cargo vessel the false impression the *Black Widow* was no threat, and their cargo was safe.

With the morning sun, the wind gradually lessened and the storm began to blow out. Without notice, heavy rain began to fall, bringing calm to the churning seas. A tiny ripple of a breeze left the Caribbean as flat as a millpond. With the drop in wind and a change of course, the *Black Widow* had gradually added sails until she ran as close to the wind as possible.

At the last moment, when it appeared the *Black Widow* was departing on her way, the captain blared the order to come about ninety degrees across the bow of the merchant ship. The French vessel maintained her course until the *Black Widow* crossed her port bow with her gun ports falling open.

As the pirate crew raced to move their cannon into firing position, Risk gave the order to strike the black flag. Quickly, the French vessel altered its course as her crew began to add sails with the hope of outrunning the pirates.

But she had been caught in the deceitful web of the *Black Widow*. The more agile ship cut through the calm seas, and quickly closed the gap with the bulky and cumbersome cargo ship. Had the captain from Marseille ran up a white flag and not tried to run, lives could have been spared.

Not now. Her fate was written in stone, and Hellsworth and Risk would not be deterred.

As sudden as fog after a storm, the *Black Widow's* entire starboard battery of cannons fired as one. The volley was so violent the deck of the pirate ship trembled as if caught in a seismic eruption.

As cannonballs crashed into the enemy, Risk pulled out his extendable spyglass in order to identify the Barquentine. Painted in gold letters on its bow was the name *Madam Blu*.

Thirty hot shots rattled the French ship and screams were already heard across the narrowing stretch of water. Wood splintered upon the impact of the lead balls. With its rigging ripped to pieces by the cannon fire, the *Madam Blu* was almost dead in the water. The pirate crew waited with grappling hooks to secure the two boats together. Each man was armed with black-powder pistols, muskets, and a variety of swords, knives, and daggers. A few held large hammers and hatchets. The lust for blood and booty flared in the crew's eyes.

The men shouted and cheered their mates on as the two vessels finally came crashing together and the pirate crew boarded the French ship like rats swarming over a carcass. The first invaders glided through the air on long ropes attached to the rigging. Others boarded on gangplanks, thrown across the gap between the two ships. Webs of rope were hung over the sides of both vessels as the pirates boarded the *Madam Blu*.

Nick Risk hastily climbed the webbing that led to the crow's nest. When he was halfway to the top, he grabbed a thick hemp rope with a grappling hook tied to the end and launched it into the air as it caught on the rigging of the cargo vessel. The rope-like muscles of his arms knotted as he lofted himself through the air and to the top of one of the mainsails of the cargo ship.

With a hay hook in hand, Nick poked it through the top of the sail and threw himself toward the deck while holding the handle tight in his fist. The white sail ripped with the weight of his body, splitting the cloth from top to bottom, while allowing him to safely descend toward the mayhem. He pulled one of his new revolvers and fired at a Frenchmen on the main deck. He charged into battle like the "Angel of Death." The crew was unprepared and almost defenseless.

two
texas nick risk

Galveston County, Texas—Some Years Earlier

WHEN YOUNG NICKY RISK came home from his chores on the family ranch, the darkest day of his life unfolded before his eyes. His family lived on a small spread some twenty-five miles inland of Galveston, Texas. His mother, father, and two brothers worked the run-down ranch as best they could. Between the rustlers and Comanche stealing livestock and the drought of the last two summers, they struggled to survive. He'd already lost two sisters to disease, but he and his brothers were hard nails, even as teenagers.

Born and bred a cowboy, Nicky had first ridden a horse at the young age of four. By the time he was ten, he was proficient with a rifle. By his twelfth birthday, he was an expert marksman. None of his skills would save his family from the tragedy that would tear at his very soul and leave him wounded for the rest of his life.

Nicky heard the gunshots and screams well before the ranch house came into view. The first hint something was wrong came from afar. Billows of black smoke could be seen just over the rise where his family resided. As he approached, he could see the flames reaching for the sky. The wind fanned the fire and carried with it the shrieks of terror.

Nicky's first instinct was to break into a run to assist, but the young boy was wise for his age. He opened the breach of his eight-gauge shotgun and checked the heavy-shot shells. Then he moved off the path and into the brush. He crouched down and began to run. His nerves were electrified as his hearing became more acute and intense. His attention grew hyper-focused and sweat broke out on his brow. His heart hammered in his chest and throbbed at his temples.

When he reached the top of the hill, he saw four men with guns. Both his brothers lay dead on the porch and his father in the middle of the yard. The only one left alive was his mother, and the outlaws were already at her as Nicky looked on in horror.

The men in the barnyard were rough-looking and unshaven. All four had scraggly hair and wore mismatched clothing. One appeared to be Mexican and another had hair the color of an over-ripe carrot. The other two looked to be brothers, twins on closer examination. Each one was dirty and unkept. Unfortunately, their weapons were in good working order, and the gun belts strapped across their chests were full of bullets.

Nicky lay behind a small outcrop of rocks, which made him invisible. He fingered the hammers on the shotgun and struggled with what to do. His instinct told him to run to help his mom, but he knew it would be hopeless. He might kill one or two of the bad men before they got him, but the outcome for his mother would not change. He would only die like the rest.

Nicky bit on his bottom lip, squeezed his eyes shut and promised his mother and God he would hunt down all four men and take their lives. Each would pay for what they had done.

"An eye for an eye and a tooth for a tooth," the young Texan whispered, reciting his father's words verbatim.

As the screams continued, the boy held his hands over his ears to block out his mother's cries. Tears streamed down his face as he swore this would be the last time he ever cried.

After a long agonizing afternoon, Nicky awoke with a start. Nightfall had descended on the terrible scene. The sound of chaos from the house and yard was gone. All he could hear was a rooster's call as the first vestiges of light began to show in the east. Shades of pink streaked the sky as the sun hid just over the horizon.

When the boy sat up, he rubbed his eyes with the heels of his hands. He blinked repeatedly and wondered if he had been dreaming. The horror of the nightmare still stood firm in his mind.

He knew better than to fall asleep in the open by himself; it was too dangerous. The fog cleared when he saw the double-barrel shotgun still clenched tightly in his white-knuckled fists. The events of the day before stood out clearly in his memory.

He swiped fresh tears from his face as reality struck. It wasn't a dream.

Fear crept back into his brain. His hearing again became hyperacute. He thumbed back the hammers on his shotgun, pushed himself to his feet, and turned toward the ranch. As he moved forward, the dread took hold, and his feet became as heavy as lead weights.

As he pushed his way through brush and bramble, he didn't notice the cuts and scratches they caused. Rivulets of blood ran down his arms. He was too fixed on what he would find when he arrived at his home.

As he walked, the images flashed before him—his dead brothers on the porch, and his father's body spread eagle in the middle of the yard. The last thing he had heard before the world went dark was the cries of his poor mother as the outlaws had their way with her. Nicky hoped she had somehow survived the ordeal, and he could still save her.

When he emerged from the tall weeds at the side of what was left of the smokehouse, he leveled the shotgun barrel as his shoulders tensed. Sweat streaked his face but there were no more tears. The boy from last night no longer existed. A young man had taken his place, determined to fulfill his promise to God and his mother.

When he walked past his father, he noted two heavy-caliber bullet holes in his chest. He squeezed his eyes tight to force back his sorrow. His brothers were on the porch with bullet holes in their heads. They stared at him with blank, empty eyes.

Surprise was etched on their pale faces and the hands of all three were empty; none of the Risk males had presented any threat to the aggressors.

His father had been a religious man. Although he owned a gun, he rarely carried it with him. A Mississippi long-rifle hung from the cabin's wall in the very back of the main room, high up in a corner nearest the kitchen. His dad thought guns were unnecessary.

The only reason Nicky had the family shotgun with him was because he had seen several rabbits on the trail to the pond the day before. He thought his family would be proud when he brought home supper for the evening. The carcasses of the hares he carried in his tote sack banged against his leg.

The only living things that remained in the yard were chickens, scratching and picking at the dirt. All the horses and cattle had been stolen, and all of the family's possessions were strewn across the ground. Obviously, the outlaws ransacked the home after killing his family. Then, they set the barn and house ablaze, but they had only partially burned.

Still, there was no sign of his mother.

As Nicky sifted through the ashes, he discovered the old Mississippi rifle still hung on the stone wall in the corner. He grabbed it and ran from the charred surroundings.

With his mother missing, he rationalized she had been taken prisoner. He searched the perimeter of the ranch house until he found their departing tracks. The young Texan lit out on foot, running to catch up with the kidnappers. He ran until he dropped, rested and began again. This time he trotted, though, pacing himself so he didn't become winded.

As he jogged, he calculated how far he could travel on foot in a full day. With his mother as extra cargo, he believed the outlaws would be slowed. He prayed they didn't stop to abuse her some more. Was she still alive?

Risk pursued the renegades for five days. Finally, on the fifth night, he spotted their campfire in the distance. He approached carefully. He pulled back the hammers on the rifle and shotgun as he moved forward into the night. His breathing was shallow. It felt like a mallet thumped in his chest with each beat of his heart.

He was hungry and covered with dust from his relentless pursuit. His only source of nourishment had been some hardtack and his canteen of water.

Of the four men, two were already in their bedrolls and snoring loudly. The other pair played cards on a blanket by the light of a brightly burning fire. Embers rose with the heat into the night air. Moths, drawn to the bright light, burst into flame.

When he reached the edge of the camp, he could make out another body under a blanket. He sensed it was his mother. At a distance, he could not tell if she was breathing or not. His heart pounded in his ears and his blood boiled with anger.

Without thinking, the young cowboy lost his composure. He cursed and swore as he charged toward the two men sitting next to the campfire. The look on their faces was something he would remember for the rest of his life. They were taken by utter surprise and immediately realized they were about to die. There wasn't a damn thing they could do to stop it.

Two blasts rang out in quick succession from the eight-gauge shotgun as flames burst from the barrel. Two gaping holes magically appeared in the outlaw's chests. They toppled over like tenpins. The rifle barked next. Nicky shot one of the men who had been asleep but awakened by the blasts of the scattergun. As the fourth man threw off his blanket and turned to look, Nicky smashed the butt of the long-rifle into his skull. It popped like a watermelon.

As he examined his handiwork, dead eyes stared up at the pulsating stars. Only the heavens breathed.

Nicky ejected two hulls from the shotgun and replaced them with fresh shells. He nudged each body with the smoking barrel, but none showed signs of life. Then, the young Texan dropped the weapon and rushed to where he hoped to find his mother. He kneeled beside her and pulled back the bloody blanket. He swallowed the bile that rose in his throat.

As soon as he lay his hands on her still body, he knew she was gone. Her skin was as cold as death and her eyes were fixed on the starlit sky. Grief washed over him as he pulled the rigid body into his arms. The kneeling boy whimpered in pain, but no more tears came as the cosmos crossed the heavens and the dark of night waned.

As he mourned, something happened to Nicky's heart. It was as if it became coated with a layer of ice. At that moment, he felt old and hardened beyond his years. The boy was forever gone, never to be seen again. All that remained was a vengeful cowboy with a penchant for violence. He was a young man with skills but no direction or plan.

Risk took everything of value from the dead outlaws, and dug a grave for his mother. As the sun breached the horizon, streaks of light sprouted up like weeds creating a prism of color.

Finished with his mother's grave, he knew he would have to return to the ranch to properly bury his father and brothers. He prayed the varmints hadn't already gotten to them. He left in such a hurry, he disregarded his responsibility to them. He felt bad for leaving them in the dirt, but how could he have known he would find his mother dead, too. He had acted on instinct, hoping to rescue her at any cost. Now, they all were dead.

three
horacio
hellsworth

London, England 1814

AS A YOUNG MAN, Horacio's mother and father were so impoverished they couldn't feed their nine children. They lived in a small one-room flat in the slums of *Saint Guiles* in London, the capital of the British Empire. At night, all slept on the floor head to toe.

When the conditions deteriorated, the children were sent to orphanages. All but Horacio acquiesced. He chose to flee the authorities before being locked up in a home for parentless children. He had heard such places were rife with wrongdoing.

Most of the young orphans became indentured, laboring for the rest of their lives. Others escaped the clutches of the government and lived on the streets. They turned to theft to survive, much like young Horacio.

Hellsworth, however, wanted more than the average life of crime. He had illusions of grandeur despite his deprived childhood. He felt the wrongs he had suffered deserved to be righted. He intended to acquire enough wealth to guarantee he would never be poor again. He sought wealth equal to that of the aristocrats of the United Kingdom. The prodigal teen honed his trade in the darkest corners of the massive English capital.

The United Kingdom's royalty boasted the most powerful navy in the world with an impressive fleet of warships. Officers always were looking for new sailors and applied devious means to acquire their crews. Frequently, children were shanghaied and forced to serve under a ship's command.

The ranks of the Royal Navy were filled with villains who had stood before judges for minor crimes and given a simple choice: join the Royal Navy or go to jail. Horacio was too crafty to be locked up, though, but his youthful inexperience allowed him to be easily tricked.

The Royal Navy employed dozens of spies who combed the London harbor district for potential sailors. Prime targets were the naïve, young men who lived on the streets. No one would notice if one or two went missing. So, they became easy prey for impressment.

Of course, being shanghaied and put to work in a press-gang meant they would receive two meals a day and shelter. So, service in His Majesty's Navy often was the lesser of two evils. Life on London's damp and foggy streets was fraught with danger, starvation and murderous predators.

Big for his age, Horacio quickly passed as a young man and was immediately noticed by the men in charge of finding more laborers for the massive Royal Navy. Always expanding, the British Navy required manpower to keep it afloat. Its need far exceeded standard inscriptions. Seafaring veterans were easily acquired, but the positions of powder monkeys and crew boys were best filled by children rescued from orphanages and the capital's streets.

As a perpetual drizzle mixed with the dense fog of the night, Horacio peered from behind a stack of wooden barrels at the man in a fancy bowler derby and black suit, vest, and frock. He had just stepped from a fancy coach at the edge of London's red-light district. A smile spread across the young thief's face as he ducked to make sure he had not been seen. A silver chain, dangling from the elite gentleman's vest pocket. It glittered under the light of a streetlamp and caught his savvy eye. Such a prize would bring several shillings to any thief who could manage to spirit it away.

During the 19th century, London grew enormously and became the world's largest city and a global metropolis of immense importance. It also boasted the world's largest port and was the heart of international finance and commerce. Accordingly, it was known as a city of opulence and where the rich could prosper.

The wealthiest were the neighbors of the most hideous poverty. The crumbs that fell from the tables of the rich proved to be delicious meals to millions of starving citizens.

Amid the opulence, pawnshops thrived. They

littered the cityscape, catering to the poor who exchanged their most valued possessions for a fraction of their value. The poor were known to pledge their raiment for a pittance, trading their last tattered bits of clothing to obtain coins to feed their families.

Along the crowded streets were the churches, where the pious prayed, and gin palaces, where the wretchedly poor drowned their sorrows.

In between was where the many victims of society's vitiated condition expiated the crimes of hunger and despair. Between the churches and gin mills is where the destitute, the elderly and the homeless fought for survival or laid down their aching heads to die in the damp, foggy streets of London.

Horacio's eyes darted from one dark corner of the prostitute ridden neighborhood to another as he carefully approached the target, unseen by the untrained observer. He moved from one shadow to another while never losing sight of the valuable prize. Every time the gentleman turned his way, the polished silver chain sparkled in the gas lamps. The young man was fixated on the priceless watch that hung from the other end of the silver links that glinted in the light.

The orphan was pinching his nose as he hid behind a pile of burlap sacks filled with garbage, when he saw his chance. The gentleman had just dropped a shiny coin, a shilling of great value. As nimbly as a cat, Horacio snatched the coin almost before the aristocrat noticed he had dropped it.

To his surprise, though, the night belonged to the shanghaies and crimps. The aristocrat and the dropped coin were part of an elaborate trap, one in which the crafty teen would not escape. A burly sailor grabbed him by the scruff of his shirt and dragged him into the carriage. The interior was dim. When Horacio's vision adjusted, he saw four more street urchins who were bound hand and mouth. Immediately, Horacio tried to break and run, but his reaction was too slow. A sailor already had a length of cable in his hands and quickly tied the boy's wrists behind his back. Then, he shoved a gag into his mouth and wrapped a bandana around his head. His escape was futile.

Hellsworth struggled against the bindings and gurgled muffled sounds, heard only by the other captured boys. Fear filled all of their eyes, and not one knew where they were being taken. The two crimps who had tied him up were undoubtedly sailors, evident by their dress and dialect.

Upon closer inspection, the man in the fancy hat and frock was not who he appeared to be either. Under his cloak, he wore the coat of an officer of the British Navy. Instantly, he knew he and the other boys were destined for impressment on one or more of the queen's vessels.

As soon as the carriage door slammed shut, the rigging on the horses clanked and the cart jerked forward. They ran through the streets of London at neck-breaking speeds, tossing the lads about the coach's interior. Horacio heard the driver lashing out with his whip at the horses as their steel-shoed hooves and the carriage's metal covered wheels ground loudly against the cobblestone streets. He imagined sparks were flying as they dashed through the night.

After what seemed like an hour, but probably wasn't more than twenty minutes, the coach abruptly pulled to a stop. The five teenagers tumbled on top of each other as a key unlocked the carriage door. When it swung open, flames leaped from torches that lined the dock in the last minutes before dawn. A nearby ship appeared to be prepared to get underway. Only a gangplank, stretching between the floating wooden pier and the towering vessel, prevented departure.

Pulled from the coach by their arms, the boys could feel the gentle movement of water beneath the dock. The smell of ocean salt filled the air. Horacio was familiar with London's harbors. They were prime spots for young thieves like himself to apply their trade. This part of the pier was unfamiliar to him, though.

He thought it odd the British officer kept glancing over his shoulder as he ushered them up the gangplank and onto the deck of the British man-of-war.

As soon as they boarded, the order was given to cast off the mooring lines and prepare to disembark. Barefoot men scurried about the deck soundlessly as if they were sneaking off to unseen hiding places.

The young captives remained bound and gagged as two of the sailors led them to the bow of the ship, where they wouldn't be in the way.

"You lads best stay put, or you'll answer to me," the gruff man warned. "I am First Mate Arthur Nightingale and I aim to make two of you boys my powder monkeys. The other three will be crew boys. You are now members of Her Majesty's Royal Navy, an assignment to be proud of."

Two rowboats, manned with eight men each, strained hard on oars as the massive ship was pulled into the harbor by long lengths of rope. The light of day was approaching as the oars churned to the cadence of a drum, and the ship slipped out to sea. Then, the boys were led below deck.

The last thing Horacio saw of England were the multicolored fangs as they shot across the sky as the sun rose against the buildings that towered across the city. To the west, stars still sparkled, and the heavens of Britain sighed one last time,

Once below, they had their gags removed and their bindings released. They were locked in what Horacio assumed was a jail cell in the bowels of the ship. The door was made of heavy timber and had a large, barred window cut into the upper half. To their backs was an open porthole. Straw mattresses lay about the floor, and an empty tin bucket sat in one corner. The stench of the room assaulted their noses, a sign to Hellsworth the carefree days of his youth were gone.

Horacio counted seven sunrises since he had been stolen from the city of his birth, but he lost track of the number of times the slop bucket they used to relieve themselves was emptied out the porthole, the only source of fresh air for the captives.

With their destiny undetermined, most of the boys trembled with fear. Not Hellsworth. He reveled in the thought of sailing the Seven Seas in a vessel of war. For an orphan who had survived the cold, damp streets of

London, this was heaven sent. Although he had been fed biscuits and water with lemon each day, it was more food than he had had on many days. He was neither cold nor wet, and he was thankful he had a mat to sleep on and a roof over his head.

"What the hell! I might one day become captain of my own vessel,"* Horacio whispered to himself.

four
the bounty hunter

Galveston County, Texas

BY THE TIME Nicky Risk was eighteen, he could shoot the wings off a fly at two hundred and fifty yards with a long-rifle. He drew his pistols with such speed, his hands were a blur. He had mastered the tools he had acquired from the very outlaws who had killed his mother, father, and brothers. He kept them as a memoir of the cruelty perpetrated by men in Texas. They also were a reminder to stand fast and never give ground, no matter what the danger. It was better to die in protest than to live as a coward. He would back down from no man.

Nicky wasn't all work and no play. Still in his late teens, he joined his buddies on occasion in silly games. It was his way of hanging on to some semblance of normality, despite the horrors of his youth.

Even though his friends were of the same age, Nicky never seemed to have as much fun as his buddies.

He preferred to focus on honing his skills so he could fearlessly put the world's wrongs right.

He also had been smitten by the lure of adventure and danger. Unconsciously, he was riddled with self-guilt. When his family was still alive, he had never wandered far beyond the outskirts of their ranch. Now, he had seen the massive Galveston docks and ships of the world that frequented them. He had a horse, weapons and a few silver coins he had seized from the outlaws. The world was at his feet.

Risk also had become a great fan of the five-cent novels of the times. He had read about such men as Daniel Boone. The young adventurers, David Crocket and Jim Bowie, were his favorites, although there were many more that kept his interest. He was drawn to their stories of adventure west of Texas and the ships that cross-crossed the globe.

Like many young men, he felt a need to prove himself. Freedom had gone to Nicky's head and he was ready to stretch his legs and expand his boundaries. His only family existed back east and had even attempted to contact him. But big cities held no allure for Risk; he preferred adventure and exploring the unknown.

"You're so danged good with those pistols and your rifle, I reckon you could become a bounty hunter or even a gunslinger," his friend, Gordo, said. "Or you could make a living as a shootist."

Willy Words was Nicky's closest friend. A red-haired boy of Scottish descent. He had light skin and a face full of freckles. His friends called him Gordo, an endearing nickname that referred to his chubby physique. Even though he was as poor as a church mouse, he always had a scrap of food in the pocket of his britches.

"How do you know so much about bounties and such?" Nicky asked.

"I read all about it in those five-cent novels," Willy replied. "You know they go after the men on the posters that say: 'Wanted Dead or Alive.' I've read the law will pay a fortune to a fella who captures one of those rascals."

Nicky's head popped straight up, and his eyes spread wide with interest. "Do you really think we could do such a thing?" he asked. "I ain't actually shot a gun at a person other than the outlaws who killed my ma and pa. That all happened in the heat of the moment."

"It beats working cows and pays more, too," Willy said. "And we don't have to actually shoot anybody. We just have to get the jump on 'em and bring the outlaw into the local authorities to collect the reward. We could get rich quick and buy supplies for our trip to California."

"I ain't especially aiming for California," Nicky said, flashing the white teeth of a smile. "I'm just wantin' to see what's west of Texas. I may even ride up to Colorado or Montana. We got the whole country at our feet, Gordo."

"Well, let's head over to the Galveston County sheriff's office and see if he don't have a wanted poster on somebody we might manage to find," Willy said. "I ain't much at trackin'. How about you?"

"If I can track a rabbit or a bobcat, I reckon I can track a loudmouthed outlaw," Nicky said with a chuckle. "Do you think we'll ever be in a five-cent novel?"

"You just never know, now do ya?" Willy said proudly.

Sure enough, when they got to the sheriff's office, they found wanted posters hanging all over a billboard and free for the taking. Nicky studied the eight or nine fliers as they considered which one would be the easiest to find and catch.

"Here's one for an outlaw who is only sixteen years old," Willy said. "It says he robbed a stagecoach. Is that bold enough for ya, Nicky? He's got a hundred-dollar reward on his head."

Risk took the yellowish paper from his friend and squinted to read the small print.

"It says his name is, Skinny Razor," Nicky said.

Words replied, "That sure is one strange name, ain't it?"

Nicky looked at his buddy, laughed and asked, "Don't you think Willy Words is an odd name too?"

"It don't seem strange to me a-tall," Willy replied. "Where does it say this Skinny Razor fella was last seen?"

"In Laredo," Nicky said. "So, he won't be there. Maybe he's working his way to the port. We're gonna have to figure out how to find him before we can catch him."

"I figure there be but three ways for him to have gone," Willy said. "One would be south and to Mexico.

If that's the case, then we can give it up right now. I ain't going over the border to chase no outlaw. Like as not, we'd be the ones who ended up in jail.

"He could head west to New Mexico, but he would have to cross the state without being seen. Then again, maybe, just maybe, he might head for Galveston to catch a ship to one of the big cities on the East Coast, where he could hide out in plain sight. Personally, that would be where I'd go."

"If I were an outlaw," Nicky pondered, "I reckon I'd head for Galveston, too. Ships are departing from the port daily, and he could be nicely entertained while he waited for his ticket out of Texas."

"Why not wait on the trail into town for this Skinny Razor to come to us?" Willy Words asked. "We could hide unseen in the brush and when he shows, jump out with our pistols pointing at him. We tie him up, take him into town and we're rich. It's as simple as that."

So, the naïve teens rode double on Nick's horse a few miles south out of Galveston. When they came to a shady tree, they dismounted, hobbled the horse and waited out of the relentless Texan sun.

After two days, they began to get hungry. They had no experience at hunting outlaws and hadn't considered it might take days, if not weeks, for him to show up on the trail. That is, if he did indeed come their way. They began to question their staying power when they got low on water.

"How long are we gonna sit here and wait on this

Skinny Razor fella?" Willy Words asked. "I'm hungry. We ain't had a bite to eat since yesterday."

Nick flashed a hard look at his friend and said, "You ain't already giving up, are ya?"

"I didn't say nothin' about giving up," Words said. "I just said I'm hungry."

"When ain't you hungry, Gordo?" Nick said, his eyes flashing with mischief. "It wouldn't do you any harm to lay down the fork for a day or two, now would it?"

"I get dizzy when I don't eat," Words replied.

The words barely slipped from Gordo's lips when they heard a horse ninny in the distance, alerting them someone was traveling their way. Forgetting their hunger, they ducked into the tall grass, trying to become as invisible as possible.

Nick and Willy waited in nervous anticipation of the unknown. Their eyes popped wide as they suddenly realized the danger they had assumed when they decided to take on such a challenge. It was too late to turn back, though. Neither was willing to retreat and lose the other's respect. They held fast and waited.

Nick pulled both of his single-shot pistols and drew back the hammers. His breathing became shallow and his heart throbbed. When he looked over at Willy, who tried unsuccessfully to show how brave he was, fear filled his friend's eyes.

The young Texan became a little unnerved when he realized two riders approached. If one was Skinny Razor, he wasn't alone.

The riders were nearly on top of the teens when the

confusion started. One of the riders had a pistol pointed at the man mounted beside him. Words were exchanged, but neither Nick nor Willy understood what was said. The threat of violence was obvious.

Willy was so afraid he thought about running, but he refused to abandon his friend, who didn't seem scared at all. He had been nervous before the two men showed up. Now, he appeared to be as calm as the day was long. This surprised Willy and bolstered his confidence.

It was a good thing, too. Without notice, Risk stood and leveled both pistols at the man with the gun.

"You best drop your weapon, mister," Nick growled with less conviction than he had hoped. "I reckon one of you two may well be Skinny Razor and I intend to take you in to the law."

The man sitting with weapon in hand didn't heed the warning. Instead, he swung the barrel of his gun toward Nick. That was when Risk pulled the triggers on both of his pistols. The weapon in his right hand bucked as a flame shot out of the barrel. The pistol in his left misfired.

The first bullet hit its mark, albeit not in a vital spot but rather in the man's shoulder. Upon impact, the stranger dropped his weapon, spun his horse around and rode off at a gallop. The second fellow just sat there with his hands in the air, like he was giving up without a fight.

"Damn," Nicky swore. "I hope that wasn't Skinny Razor who just run off."

"No, I'm Skinny Razor," the man with his hands in

the air said. "That fella you just shot was a US Marshal."

The shock on the teenagers' faces was almost comical. They looked at the wanted outlaw in total disbelief. How could they possibly have shot a US Marshal?

Skinny Razor had limp, greasy hair that fell nearly to his shoulders and was always falling in his face. At five feet four, both Nick and Willy towered over him. His wiry, muscular frame indicated he might have catlike movements.

"We shot a marshal?" Willy asked in disbelief.

"We've been hunting you for a couple days, Mr. Razor," Nicky said, a bit confused.

"It looks like you got me, but now I reckon the marshal will head for Galveston and bring back more law to deal with the three of us," Skinny said.

Nick could tell Skinny wasn't the brightest man in Texas. He looked much younger than expected and nothing like a man with a bounty on his head. Then again, Nicky and Willy weren't typical bounty hunters.

"Can I put my hands down now?" Skinny Razor asked with a hint of a smile at the corner of his mouth.

Risk consented, made an ugly groan and spat into the dirt.

"We must be as dumb as a dog's foot," Nick grumbled.

"And as dull as rusted iron," added Willy.

"If you two don't decide to do somethin' other than flappin' your jaws, we're all gonna end up as dead as doornails," Razor said with a glimmer of hope in his eyes. "Whatcha say we hightail it out of here?"

the dark ship

Port Galveston, Texas

NICKY AND WILLY suddenly realized things had gotten completely out of hand. Now, they would be on wanted posters and have bounties on their heads, all because of an innocent mistake by two amateurs. It also became apparent they never should have ventured into such a serious profession without investigating the risks involved.

The path was one frequently chosen by teenage boys who were desperate to be seen as men. In light of their action, they had to flee. They mounted their horses and rode like the wind for Port Galveston with Skinny Razor in tow.

Their only chance of escape, it seemed, was to board a ship that hopefully would transport them somewhere safe, either across the Gulf of Mexico or up the East Coast of America. They knew they had to get far away from Texas and the long arm of the justice system.

As soon as they arrived at the port, they abandoned their horses at the hitching rail of a tavern and rushed to disappear among the crowded docks. They believed their time for escape was short, because shooting a US Marshall was a grave offense. Lawmen already could be in pursuit. They had to find a ship as quickly as possible. Ideally, it would be a vessel in the process of departing the harbor and ready to set sail on the high seas.

The three young men darted from one shadow to another, making sure no one caught more than a fleeting glance of them. They feared the alarm would already have gone out, and the first place lawmen would search was the docks. As they made their way to the very end of the huge wharf, they spotted a small ship that appeared ready to set sail. Conveniently, the two-masted craft was moored with no other vessels nearby. It was as if it were in some sort of isolation from the rest of the ships in the harbor.

As they moved closer, nobody seemed to pay the three boys much mind. Finally, Nicky picked up a box from a stack on the pier, lifted it to his shoulder, and followed other dockworkers up the gangplank and onto the weathered vessel. Willy and Skinny scrambled to grab more cargo and followed the cowboy. Most dock-workers were Black. But there was a sprinkling of poor White crackers mixed in among the laborers, allowing the trio to pass unchallenged.

As soon as their feet hit the ship's deck, they

dropped their cargo and ran for the stern where a tender swung, suspended from cables below the ship's transom. Nick reached over and pulled back the canvas tarp and climbed inside. He was followed by his two friends. They pulled the brown canvas cover tight and hoped nobody was watching.

"What are we gonna do now?" Willy asked.

"Shut up, fool," Nicky whispered. "If they find us, they might throw us overboard. We've got to stay out of sight until we can jump ship at the next port."

"How long do you think that will be?" Skinny asked.

"I'm hungry," Willy proclaimed. "What are we gonna do for food?"

Nicky looked over at his friend and shook his head in bafflement. "Don't you think about anything other than food?" he said. "We'll wait till dark and see what we can find to eat and drink. We'll have to be careful, though."

The three boys lay silent in the small boat, used to take the ship's captain ashore when anchored. They were careful not to make any noise, for fear of being caught. Shooting a US Marshal most definitely could result in a lengthy prison sentence, if not three hangings. So, their lives depended on them remaining undiscovered.

It wasn't long before they heard the order for the mooring lines to be cast off. They felt the ship gently roll from one side to the other as the crew began to raise the sails. Their escape to the Gulf of Mexico and freedom beyond had begun. All three of the stowaways were hungry and scared to death, a fact they tried to hide from each other. They also shared a sense of joy, too. They had saved themselves, even if only for the moment.

"What kind of ship is this?" Willy asked as he lifted the edge of the canvas to peek out. "All the cargo I saw was food stock and water. What do you think they carry on the decks below?"

"What difference does it make what kind of ship it is?" Risk replied.

"It could be a pirate ship," Skinny whispered and peeked out from under the tarp. His eyes searched far and wide.

"There ain't hardly any pirates around anymore," Willy said. "We best worry about the captain of this ship finding out we be stowaways."

Night came as they reached the Gulf of Mexico, and the gentle sway of the ship was magnified. With the swell, the dingy at the stern, where the stowaways hid, swayed haphazardly beneath the transom.

"I think I'm gonna be sick," Razor said as his face turned green. "I've never been at sea before."

"None of us have been on a ship before," Nicky said. "Just make sure you don't get sick in here, or we'll all end up with a bad stomach. Vomiting is contagious."

"I feel fine," Willy said. "But I'm so hungry my stomach is growling."

When the ship finally went quiet, the three boys lifted the edge of the canvas cover and looked out. Only a skeleton crew remained on the deck. Their silhouettes barely were discernible in the dark, moonless evening. The boys made their way down the vessel's port side, ducking behind a hatch when a sailor walked by. Sweat streamed down their faces, but hunger outweighed their fear.

Willy's hands trembled visibly as he advanced, but his need for food bolstered his bravery to continue on. When they came to a large hatch that led down to the bowels of the creaking vessel, they hid in the shadows until they could descend without being seen.

Finally, they ducked into the hatch and scurried down the steps that led to the guts of the ship. The first deck they encountered was the gun deck with a dozen cannons. All up and down the lower deck, men slept on bedrolls strung out in a line.

The trio hesitated for a moment as their eyes adjusted to the dim light of the lower deck. Oil lamps that hung from the ceiling beams swung back and forth with the swell of the sea. The ship's planks creaked. Sounding like a small village of snoring souls, every man appeared to be sound asleep. The unloading and loading of the goods prior to departure had worn the crew out. All had to work double-time. Slumber came easily as the ship rocked them in its arms.

Nicky nodded and pointed to the next set of steps that led even deeper into the ship's belly. As the boys made their way down another flight, the wooden stairs creaked so loud they feared the sound would awaken the crew. But nobody stirred.

When they arrived at the next deck, the galley was immediately to their left. Willy was the first to discover the entrance, lifting his head and letting the aroma of last night's supper fill his nostrils. Nicky and Skinny were right behind him.

"Quick now," Nicky whispered as his eyes gaped and darted all around. "Grab those loaves of bread and that wheel of cheese. Fill the canteens with water. Move quickly before someone catches us and makes us walk the plank."

Willy grabbed a small burlap sack from a shelf and began shoving long bars of bread and round disks of cheese inside. Each time he grabbed some food, he took a bite of whatever it was. Satisfaction glowed on his face. Even in the face of danger, Gordo found food more important than his own safety.

When they made their way out of the galley, Nicky looked around the corner to make sure nobody was about. It appeared this deck was used for cargo, but it seemed to be mostly vacant. That was when he noted the long strings of chains attached to the beams of the hull. Shackles dangled at the ends. The revelation stopped the boys dead in their tracks.

As their eyes followed the long line of chains, they saw at the very end lay two bodies, apparently asleep. Shackles were attached to their ankles. When light glistened from the whites of two pairs of eyes, their hearts were filled with apprehension.

"Shush," Nicky hissed as he held his index finger to his lips.

The trio carefully made their way to the back of the vessel, where they found two colored boys, both teens who apparently were meant to be traded or sold as slaves. Each of the three stowaways came from poor backgrounds, but they knew nothing of slavery.

The fear in the slaves' eyes made Nick and his friends pause. Risk said, "We ain't here to harm you boys. We be stowaways ourselves."

The teenager nearest them asked, "What are y'all doing on a slave ship? Don't you know what'll happen to you White boys if they catch ya?"

"We had to run from the law in Galveston and this ship was the only one we saw we could sneak onto," Nick replied, wide-eyed.

"That's because nobody in their right mind would board a slave ship," the black boy said. "My name's Wishbone, and this is my brother Hambone."

"Where are we headed?" Skinny asked. "I plan to jump ship as soon as it docks."

"We be headed for Bridgetown in Barbados," Wishbone replied. "We was sent back because nobody wanted to buy us. The folks purchasing slaves back in Texas and Matamoros figured we was too small, I reckon. The ship is sailing back to collect another load of bodies to sell in Mexico and America."

"Damn," Nicky said as he realized the boys were nearly his age. Without thinking twice, he added, "You fellas wanna go with us?"

Wishbone looked at Nicky wishfully, but Hambone replied. "What about these?" he asked and pointed to his shackles.

"How long will it take us to sail to Bridgetown?" Nicky asked as he shot a glance at the stairs and their escape.

"A week, maybe two," Wishbone replied. "I ain't sure as I lost track of time on the way north."

"How are we gonna stay in that little boat for so long?" Willy asked.

"Would you prefer we be down here with Wishbone and his brother?" Nicky asked. "Don't worry, boys. We'll get those chains off of ya, and you can come with us. Just wait and be patient. I'll get all of us out of this."

six
powder monkeys

The Atlantic Ocean Aboard a British Vessel

BEING a young powder monkey on a warship meant they would be in the midst of battles when enemies were encountered. They were considered a level above ordinary crew boys because they faced considerably more danger. If and when an adversary was confronted, they were charged with supplying ammunition for the dozens of cannons on the *HMS Howe*.

A powder monkey manned the artillery deck. Their chief role was to ferry gunpowder from the powder magazine in the ship's hold to the artillery pieces at the gunports. Children did this to minimize the risk of fires and explosions. Most powder monkeys were ten to sixteen years of age. They were selected for their speed and height; shorter helpers could move quickly in the limited spaces between decks.

Due to their shorter stature, they remained hidden

behind the ship's gunwale, which kept them from getting shot by enemy sharpshooters. Just like the orphans with Horacio, they held no official naval rank.

Crew boys were used for everything from cleaning the officers' clothing to delivering meals from the galley to the officers' mess hall. They even carried food and drink to the captain's quarters. Usually, the wards were boys, but that was not always the case. Occasionally young girls and women would work aboard a ship, but they were limited to the duties of crew boys. Often, they were abused by the officers. The powder monkeys were normally males with better physical capabilities.

Horacio and Donk Magee were immediately selected for the job of supplying the cannons with gunpowder. Even though Horacio was too tall for the position, he had no trouble moving heavy barrels of powder from the ammunition hold to the gun bays. Donk was reasonably short, but he had the strength of an ox, which made him the perfect choice for the position.

Donk had sailed from the Australian penal colony to London, intending to catch another ship for New York and eventually San Francisco. He had planned to join the Sydney Ducks Gang that commanded the streets of Northern California's port. His plans had been interrupted by the Royal Navy and their grimes. His neck was nearly as thick as his head, and his massive shoulders drooped from the bulk of muscle. He didn't move as quickly as Horacio, but he was a big, blonde and as loyal as a puppy.

They were separated from the other three newly

pressed teens and taken to the cannon master to learn their responsibilities. Horacio was excited about learning something new, especially when it involved cannons. The young Englishman was delighted with his position and gave his instructor his utmost attention.

Horacio didn't mind being discovered and pressed into duty. Had they asked him to join, he would have gladly volunteered. He instantly became enamored with the sea and everything about it, especially its boundlessness. He could look in all directions, and the water was endless.

Whatever lay over the horizon would surely be an adventure worthy of the voyage.

He worked hard every day, marking the quickest paths to the ammo-dump and the forty cannons. The artillery was positioned on two decks. Donk Magee would take care of the lower deck and Horacio the upper one.

Magee was not as astute as Horacio, but he was a dedicated follower. He took to the Londoner instantly and became a loyal friend. He was reasonably easy to instruct, and the heavy barrels of gunpowder and the cannonballs were like feathers to the beast of a man. He never seemed to anger, but he could nearly take a man's head off if he struck him with one of his massive paws.

As a boy, Donk had been imprisoned in Australia, where he had learned the ways of violent men. Great Britain had transformed the entire island into a prison. Many of the convicts caught ships to America once they had served their sentences. The last place they wanted to go was back to the United Kingdom. Of course, some men stayed and called Australia home. Donk could only afford passage to London. From there, he hoped to catch another affordable ship to America. His plans were thwarted by the Royal Navy's grimes.

At night, the boys slept in the brig, just like when they were shown aboard the ship. Horacio suspected it was to protect them from the sailors who might harm or take advantage of them.

One of the boys, Jack Fury, was from Great Britain. He was from the Cornwall region of south England and had escaped the detention center for wayward children before slowly making his way to London.

He had lived by the ocean all his life and had often worked on fishing boats from his village. Of the five orphans, he was the most versed in maritime matters. His course and cracked hands told the story of a life of labor aboard ships, where he frequently pulled icy nets from the freezing cold waters of the North Sea.

Jack Fury was only five feet six, but he already had powerful arms, and the muscles in his back rippled as his hands drew the heavy nets toward the boats. He had been born with bald patches on his head, so he had shaved it bare at an early age. It made him look older and menacing, especially as he approached manhood.

Aldo Rey was a Spanish-born Basque with limp black hair and a smooth face, barely marred by a trace of a mustache. An orphan like so many others, he appeared to have come from mixed blood, but he never knew his parents. He had a slight build, but was as fast as spit with his fists or a knife.

The fifth member of the small group of sequestered children intentionally stayed apart from the rest. While the other four bonded quickly, they suspected their counterpart was standoffish because he considered himself better than the rest. Upon closer inspection, Horacio noticed the boy was a female in the guise of a male.

The realization came as an absolute surprise to the other four boys. They were left speechless, especially when they discovered under the dirt and grime was a beautiful young woman. Her body was just beginning to blossom, and all the young men immediately formed a crush on her.

Celestia Fox worked as a crew boy, even though she was secretly a girl. She hid the fact by dressing like the others and acting bold and bossy. That latter attitude seemed to come naturally to her. Inside the tattered clothing was a tall, blue-eyed, blonde-haired beauty. As the days passed, the boys became more and more protective of Celestia, and all agreed to guard her secret with their lives.

Eventually, the day arrived when the crew was called to their battle stations. None of the young men were as prepared as Hellsworth. He reveled at the idea of a battle with another ship. His curiosity and imagination ran rampant in anticipation. Standing at the gunwale, he intended to show his bravery and make a mark. Maybe the first mate would put him in charge of his own cannon.

The ship was buzzing with activity as men ran the decks' length or climbed high up into the riggings. The cannon ports were opened, and the big guns were stuffed with powder and charges of nuts, bolts and scraps of metal. Other batteries used solid balls that would tear the masts to pieces when they hit. The rest of the crew prepared to board the ship.

When Horacio looked out the gunport at the enemy they intended to attack, he was surprised to see a black flag atop its mast. This was the first pirate ship he had ever seen, and something about it hypnotized him. He was so mesmerized, he forgot to do his job. First Mate Nightingale slapped him in the back of the head and urged him to action. When Horacio looked up at the man, he saw cruel eyes below jet-black hair and a malicious grin that twisted his face grotesquely. His eyes filled with hatred every time he looked at the boy from the streets of London.

Maybe that was why the first mate despised the young orphan so. Of course, Nightingale treated all of the crew boys and powder monkeys with disdain. He saw them all as thieves who robbed rich men. Horacio had been treated harshly all of his life. So, it was just more of the same.

One day, I'll have my own ship, and then if I meet First Mate Arthur Nightingale again, it will be to a different tone, Horacio thought.

When the order came for the battery of some forty cannon to be fired, the roar was deafening. Horacio's ears rang, and his head throbbed. The air smelled strong of cordite and the visibility on the under deck was hazy from the smoke. Between barrels of gunpowder and lead, Horacio glanced at the action every chance he got. His heart raced with excitement.

When the pirate ship returned fire, bits of red-hot lead seared the air and ripped at the sails. Wood splintered when the heavy shot hit its mark. Both ships continued the assault, reloading each weapon as fast as they could. Screams came for more gunpowder and Horacio charged across the deck for more ammo. That was when the young powder monkey was lifted off his feet by a blast that hit just beside his leg. He was tossed through the air and slammed against the hull.

The impact was devastating. Hot lead sliced through Horacio's leg as if it were made of thin parchment. Splinters of wood filled the air, and one pierced Hellsworth's eye. Blood flowed down his cheek, but he felt no pain. In shock, he staggered forward, tried to step on his missing leg and fell to the deck. He lost consciousness and drifted into a feverish coma.

Amid the battle, Horacio was tended to quickly by the ship's surgeon. He heated a large clever until it was red hot, and pressed up against Horacio's stump, severed just above the knee. It cauterized the wound and saved his life.

His injured eye turned gray and swelled. It stared at nothing as Horacio fought against a life-threatening fever that raged for days. Eventually, his temperature eased. When he finally opened his eye, he thought he was in the presence of an angel.

Instead, it was Celestia. She had stayed by his side for days as the fever tried to steal his life. With his head resting in her lap, Horacio tried to blink away the dizziness and fog. When he smiled ever so slightly, he winced and his dry, cracked lips bled.

He was pale and somewhat emaciated after days of fever and no food. Celestia squeezed a moist cloth over Horacio's mouth to rehydrate him one drop at a time.

With his fever abated, Horacio began to show healing signs. His eye twinkled his appreciation for the nurse who oversaw his recovery, and he still was not fully aware of his injuries. It was something Celestia knew she had to disclose, but she sorely dreaded the chore. Horacio wasn't awake for long. He again fell into a deep sleep, exhausted by days of sickness.

Hellsworth drifted in and out of consciousness for two more days before the fever set him completely free. Celestia was dozing beside him when he sat up for the first time. It felt good to be alive, even though he had no idea how badly he had been wounded.

While she lay still, Horacio tried to blink away the sleep and deep fog that had embraced him for days. He immediately felt the hole where his right eye had been. When his left eye strayed downward, he noted the bloody bandages on his stump and realized how badly he had been injured.

When Celestia finally stirred, Horacio winced and said, "It looks like I didn't fare too well in that scrap, now does it?"

His nurse didn't know how to reply, especially as Horacio seemed to take his injuries in stride. He acted like it was just another day.

"You took a direct hit to your knee from a cannon-ball," Celestia said. "Luckily, it didn't have a charge in it. It severed your leg but made a clean job of it. First Mate Nightingale said it was just bad luck. A fragment of wood from the blast is what pierced your face. It damaged your eye beyond repair."

Horacio shook his head and said, "I've seen folks worse off. I guess I'll look the part when I become the captain of a pirate ship."

Celestia immediately whipped her head around to make sure nobody heard what Horacio said. Concern etched across her face.

"You could get a hundred lashes for talking like that," Celestia whispered as she looked around again. "With the state you're in, I doubt you could withstand such a whipping."

"I'll live! At least I think I'll live," Horacio said as he managed a smile. "I doubt a sledgehammer could put me down."

And it was true. No matter what they did to Horacio, he bounced back and asked for more. From that day, the gang called him Horacio "Hammer" Hellsworth.

During the next days, the first mate was on his case daily. Why he had it in for the young Londoner, Horacio had no idea. But he didn't plan to allow the situation to continue. As soon as he got his strength back, he intended to confront anyone who mistreated him; he vowed to take no more abuse.

Donk Magee came by bearing gifts when Horacio began to move around. Nobody had treated Donk as fairly as Hammer, and he regarded him so highly he would do anything for the man.

"I made you something, Hammer," Donk said with his hands behind his back. When he brought them forward, he revealed a piece of teakwood he had shaped to replace his friend's missing leg.

"I found this piece of wood in the back of the ammo hold, and I stole a rifle from the weapons depot," Donk whispered, unsure of his own words. "Ya see, I carved it for you and all. If you look at the bottom, you'll see the barrel of the rifle. All you have to do is lift your leg and pull this wire and it'll fire."

Horacio grinned and said, "Why, that's as fine a gift as I've ever received. What's that carved into the side?"

"It's a sledgehammer," Donk replied with a smile. "On the other side, I carved your new nickname, Hammer. I don't know my letters, but Celestia showed me on paper. I think it's fittin' for a captain."

Horacio adjusted the black leather patch that covered his right eye, a gift Celestia made for him. He blinked away the single tear that formed in his good eye and thanked his friend. He was at mid-sentence when he saw something move inside of Donk's pockets.

Horacio's frowned and asked, "What's in your pocket, Donk?"

Donk Magee reached inside his jacket with a massive paw and pulled out a plump white rat.

"It's my new pet. I got it off the pirate ship," he said. "The Captain is pleased as punch over the spoils we confiscated from the pirates. And I got Pepe. He's a prince in the rat kingdom."

seven
celestia fox

The Irish Countryside

CELESTIA FOX WAS BORN in the beautiful countryside of Ireland. Her parents were potato farmers all their lives, as were their forefathers. That was until disease hit their crops and they failed season after season. When the famine hit the country in earnest, every family that could left in any manner possible.

Irish folks with money purchase passage on ships to North and South America. Those less fortunate fled to England or Europe, where at the very least they could feed their families.

The Fox clan were dirt poor. Even though they attempted to sell their farm, there were no takers. Half of the farms in Ireland were for sale. So, they headed for London, where they hoped to find work. There were no jobs to be had in Dublin.

The group totaled twelve, plus Celestia. The

women rode in the carts they once used to collect their harvest back on their abandoned farm. They were drawn by three aging draft horses and stacked with all their meager belongings. Celestia, her aunts, and her cousins rode on top of a stack of furniture and wooden boxes. Little did they know the forests they traveled were heavily populated with bandits.

On the fourth night of their journey, the highwaymen struck. They had little to nothing of any real value to steal, but one man's rubbish is another man's treasure. They were robbed of their horses, carts, and all of their belongings; they were left penniless. They had neither provisions nor possessions.

Celestia's father was so distraught, he disappeared that very same night without saying a word to anybody. He ran in shame, abandoning his family because he was unable to provide for them. The next day her mother took her life, unable to cope with the family's dire situation and her husband's departure.

What family was left, listlessly made their way toward the British capital. One by one, family members seemed to vanish, fearing an uncertain future.

Three days later, they made a rough camp for the night. They slept on the hard, cold ground, using their tattered coats and scarves to keep themselves from freezing to death. When Celestia awoke the next morning, she found herself alone. All had stolen away into the night. She assumed her aunts and uncles left her in desperation, opting to attend to the needs of their own children.

Only in her teens, Celestia was hopelessly lost. She had little sense of direction and no money or valuables. She owned nothing more than the clothing on her back, and they were hand-me-downs from her male cousins.

When the truth of her situation sunk in, she dropped to the ground and sobbed. The hot tears of fear and frustration burned warm streaks down her cold cheeks. She sobbed so hard, it caused her to struggle for air. Finally, she reached deep down inside herself and mustered a fistful of resolve. She promised herself she would never give up like her father and mother had. No matter what the costs, she would somehow survive and get to London. Only then would she consider allowing her thoughts to wander to the future.

All alone, she moved cautiously and managed to go unnoticed until she finally reached her destination, the British capital. The size of the city and the masses of people overwhelmed her. Of course, London had its fair share of vampire-like villains who prey on helpless, lost females. Unfortunately, Celestia was no exception.

When she reached the outskirts of London, she was snatched off the street in short order and spirited away to Saint Guiles and the brothels. As luck would have it, on her first night in the city, she was seized by the same gang of cutthroats who shanghaied Horacio, Jack Fury, Donk Magee, and Aldo Rey. It saved her from falling into the clutches of vile men who would use and abuse her in the worst ways imaginable.

While being kidnapped by Her Majesty's Royal Navy was a blessing, Celestia was faced with another challenge. Dressed in her bedraggled hand-me-downs, it was presumed she was a teenage boy. Therefore, she had to play the role in order to avoid further indignities.

eight
the great escape

The island of Barbados, Caribbean Sea

ON THE NIGHT before the slave ship arrived at the Barbados port of Bridgetown, Nicky went down to the galley for food and to search for something to free Wishbone and Hambone from their chains. He filled his tote sack with grub and began to rummage for something to use against the shackles.

Lo-and-behold, he found the hammer and chisel the slavers must have used to do what he sought to undo. Nicky believed there was strength in numbers. So, it was imperative to add the two young slaves to their ranks.

On their own, the stowaways easily could be mistaken for street urchins or thieves. With a band, they could demand respect and pose a threat against harassment and avoid trouble.

He had no idea what he would do next. Since the day he and Willy decided to become bounty hunters, it seemed they had gotten caught up in a twister and were randomly thrown into the unknown.

Risk was running on pure instinct, and he intended to keep moving forward until they found a safe haven. He had no idea where Barbados was or what to expect from a place so far away from Texas. Wishbone said the island was a British possession and located somewhere south of Florida. It made him keenly aware they would have to steer clear of any English soldiers, who cared little for Americans.

From the galley, Nicky peeked down the length of the lower deck toward the brothers, who remained chained at the far end. The only light on the lower deck was a lamp hanging in the galley hallway, which swung from side to side as the ship sailed south.

Nicky had to feel his way through the darkness to take hammer and steel to the shackles. Twice, he slammed the hammer on his thumb, biting his tongue so as not to yell out in pain. In the end, he got them free, even though he was sure he had made enough noise to wake the dead.

Risk broke off two chunks of cheese and pulled a loaf of bread in two for the skinny black teens. The brothers, who survived on meager rations, gobbled down the food immediately. They both had curly hair cut tight to their heads. Both were relatively small, but fibered muscle was obvious under their ragged clothing. Long days in the cotton fields left them fit and healthy, even if they didn't seem physically threatening.

Now we're five, and a formidable force! Nicky thought to himself. *We just might make it.*

The brothers followed Nicky back to the small rowboat. They climbed inside and pulled the canvas tight over them. The quarters were close, but they knew soon they would moor at the Bridgetown docks and could escape into the night.

The five boys lay as quiet as they could as the ship slowly moved into the port. Finally, when they felt the vessel bang into the dock, they heard the crew spring into action and secure the craft. The crew shaped the ends of the mooring lines into bowline knots and secured the ship to the bollards before they swung the gangplank into place.

They had sailed into Bridgetown late in the afternoon, and within an hour of their docking darkness began to engulf them. The pier shone bright with giant torches. Flames danced as black smoke drifted into the sky. There were many ships in the harbor, but most were anchored in the bay under a moonless sky. As soon as it became dark, the five lads used the pulleys and cables to lower the rowboat to the still water. Then they silently rowed away from the ship and searched for a safe spot to land.

"Will they come after you boys?" Nicky softly asked the brothers. "I reckon you got owners or some such thing. We ain't well versed on slavery."

"Slave owners don't like runts much, as they figure we can't do as much work as the others. They be mistaken on that account," Hambone said. "My brother and I can outwork most anybody we've met."

"Is that a fact?" Nicky asked as he smiled at his new friends. "Now you fellas are as free as we are, which ain't saying much until we can get to someplace safe."

"It's a heck of a lot better than where we were before." Hambone laughed. "There ain't a damned thing pleasant about being slaves."

They skirted the coast until they saw a sandy beach where they could row ashore. Nicky brought a big meat cleaver from the galley, which he used to chop a hole in the bottom of the rowboat. It sank out of sight but near the water's edge.

"Why did you sink the boat?" Skinny Razor asked. "Now, we don't have any way to get off this island."

"That boat is much too small for us to set out on our own," Risk replied. "If a gale would blow up, we'd be swamped or overturned. I reckon we stand a better chance of finding a way off this island if we stay close to the port. If we had left the boat here, they would know to come looking for us in town. With the boat sunk, they may well think we were foolish enough to try to sail away, or maybe they will figure the tender got lost at sea. I don't know what they'll do when they find Wishbone and Hambone gone."

"We better find a place to hide," Hambone said. "I don't think they'll run us down as they don't figure my brother and me are worth much. But men of color can't just go walking around on this island unless they belong to somebody. This is where they warehouse black folks to ship off to different places to be sold. Men and women, like Wishbone and me, be coming and going all the time."

As they moved inland through dense vegetation,

Nick, Willy, and Skinny were amazed at how green things were. In Texas, the only thing they ever saw was rocks, desert sand and hot country. Oh, sure, it was hot enough on the island, but green was everywhere. They could hear animals rustling in the brush as they searched for someplace to hide for the time being.

Willy filled his poke sack with fruit that hung from the trees they passed. He even devoured a half dozen bananas along the way. When they got to a clearing, they noticed the moon had escaped cloud covering and gave them enough light to continue their flight to safety.

"I might just like this island," Willy said as he shoved a small butter banana into his mouth. "I never seen a place with so much food right there on the trees for the pickin'."

"Stop holding us up, or we'll be seen before we get Wishbone and Hambone to a safe hiding place," Nicky said. "We'll leave Skinny behind with the brothers, while Willy and me go into town and ask around for a ship. I'd fancy sailing to South America, I think."

"I wonder what the food is like in South America," Willy asked as he cut off a slice of papaya and devoured it.

Finally, they found a natural spring in a small clearing in the middle of the jungle. A sliver of the moon reflected white in the still pond. Crickets chirped and animals slithered through the vegetation. The dense jungle canopy opened and allowed the moon and stars to illuminate the area.

The island provided more than they had imagined.

Of course, the orphans didn't know much about the islands or the Caribbean Sea. They knew less of islands like Cuba and Barbados that catered to the slave trade. Nicky, Willy, and Skinny had never been beyond the borders of Texas and their education was just as limited. The same went for Wishbone and Hambone. They had sailed the seas, but their education extended no further than the cotton fields.

When Nick and Willy finally walked into Bridgetown, they were amazed. The people spoke English but with a heavy British accent. The place was inhabited with all colors of people who were dressed in bright, printed clothing.

"If this place is anything like Galveston, there be hurdy-gurdy houses near the docks. They say it's the same in ports the world over," Willy said. "Sailors have an itch to scratch after months at sea. If we visit the taverns, we might find a ship to sign on with."

nine
bridgetown, barbados

Bridgetown, Barbados

HORACIO HELLSWORTH, known as Hammer, sat in the dim corner of a sleazy Bridgetown tavern and watched the young American and his chubby friend walk in. The cowboy, obviously the leader of the two, had an air about him that was palatable. It was felt by all as soon as he entered. It was as if some unseen force drew the occupants' attention in his direction. The tavern was mostly populated by people who walked on the darker side of life, much like the orphans.

It was as though they were drawn together like magnets. Nick's eyes immediately were drawn to the shadowy corner where Horacio sat and observed the comings and goings of sailors, officers and ladies of the night.

Horacio Hellsworth finally had had enough of the first mate's poor treatment. He jumped ship and was wanted for desertion by the British Navy. He was joined by a loyal group of friends. Celestia Fox, Donk Magee, Aldo Ray, and Jack Fury followed him wherever he went. They roamed freely because Bridgetown was bustling with people and far too busy to pay any mind to a young group of scallywags.

To avoid running into anyone from the *HMS Hue*, they hid until she again set out to sea. Horacio, surrounded by his small crew, quickly decided he was going to steal one of the ships in the harbor so they could become pirates. He happened to be looking for more crewmembers to man such a vessel and it appeared that two such men were standing before him.

Bridgetown was frequented by sailors from all over the world. The exceptions were vessels that sailed flags of countries that were at war with the British Empire. So, there was always an array of boats and ships docked in the harbor. How many men he would need to maneuver such a ship was something the young Londoner had yet to decipher. Of course, the size of the crew would depend on the type of vessel he was able to steal.

He convinced his fellow crewmembers who worked as powder monkeys and crew boys to join his gang. So, he had five of the men he would need to set sail if the right opportunity presented itself.

The cowboy and his pudgy friend looked bold and out of place. Horacio was positive, they would be candidates to join him on his pirate adventure. Even his fat friend would be welcome. Horacio remained in the shadows as his eyes carefully followed the two as they strolled to the bar.

"Two beers, please," Willy said as the barman looked at the two Americans dubiously.

"Are you old enough to drink?" the barman said, taunting the young men.

Nick reached into his jacket pocket, pulled out a coin and flicked it onto the counter. "Does that make us old enough to drink in your tavern?" he asked.

The man's demeanor immediately changed, and a smile stretched across his face. He quickly filled two mugs with warm beer for the young men.

"Here you go, gentlemen." The barman grinned. "I'll let ya know when your money runs out."

Nick and Willy sipped their drinks and let their eyes scan the pub. People of every color, race, and creed were there, along with a few British soldiers. They weren't from the Royal Navy, so the boys paid them no heed.

Nick didn't understand half of the languages or dialects spoken in the packed and noisy tavern. Women, clothed in bright pastel prints, moved among the patrons to deliver bottles of rum and large pitchers of beer.

An inebriated customer grabbed one of the girls by the backside. She didn't hesitate. She spun around and punched the zealous client in the mouth, knocking him clear off his chair. With no regard for the patron's embarrassment, the crowd roared its approval. The reaction was an example of the camaraderie that existed among seafaring men whose faces were burned dark from the sun and whose hands were cracked and calloused from working riggings soaked with saltwater.

When Nick's eyes reached the corner where

Horacio sat, he recognized the fiery look he attracted. He wasn't surprised when the brash Londoner curled his index finger, indicating for the Americans to come to his table. Nick looked from Horacio to Willy and back again. He shrugged his shoulders, nudged his friend to follow and headed to the tavern's darkest corner.

"Have a seat, Yanks," Horacio said with a smile as he pushed out a chair for Risk. "What brings two American cowboys to a place like Barbados?"

"How is it you know so much about Americans?" Nick asked.

"My name is Horacio 'Hammer' Hellsworth," he said as he proffered his hand and smiled. "The cowboy hat and boots are a dead giveaway, mate."

Nick looked the Englishman up and down. He quickly decided he looked more like a pirate than an average sailor. He lacked only a parrot to sit on his shoulder to match the description in the five-cent novels he read back in Texas. They glamorized the pirate lifestyle.

"Yes, sir, a man wears his life on his chest in most jobs," Horacio said. "You men wouldn't be looking for a ship, would ya?"

Both Willy and Nick's eyes popped as wide as saucers. They couldn't believe their ears. A ship was precisely what they were looking for. When Hammer offered them an opportunity, he wasn't completely straightforward with his explanation.

"We don't have any skills at workin' on ships, but we learn fast," Nick replied. "There's just one problem.

There's three more of us. My name is Nick Risk, and this is my friend, Willy Words."

"And how did the five of you get to Barbados?" Horacio asked.

At first, Nick fell silent, calculating the liability of telling the truth. He knew if he lied, it could backfire in the future and blow their chances of finding a ship to eventually take them back to America but not necessarily Texas, where they were wanted men. They were in a strange land without friends. This could be their only chance to solve their most pressing problem: securing a safe place where they could stay out of sight for a while.

"We came here on a ship," Nick said. In a whisper, he added, "We were stowaways."

"On what ship?" Horacio asked, also in a whisper.

"We didn't catch the name," Nicky replied. "It was a...ah...a slave ship. But it was nearly empty when we snuck aboard. They must have been shipping black folks from here to Galveston, Texas, and Matamoros, Mexico."

He could see Horacio's eyes narrow as he glanced across the saloon to make sure nobody was listening. Then he beckoned the two men to lean in closer.

Horacio whispered, "I aim to captain a pirate ship." Then he waited breathlessly as he stared at the two men to see their reaction.

Neither seemed to be offended. Instead, they appeared more interested as they leaned closer to hear more of what he had to say.

"Have you men ever been in trouble with the law?"

Horacio asked. "If you have, now is your chance to put things right."

"We stowed away to escape a marshal in Texas," Willy replied, provoking Nick to elbow him in the side. Horacio's eyebrows rose, and he smiled again.

"Just like the rest of us," Horacio said. "I have another four men with me. If we join up, we would be ten and maybe just enough to make my plan work."

"So, you don't mind if our colored friends come along?" Nick carefully asked as he searched Horacio's face for a reaction.

The young Londoner laughed and whispered, "There is no race or color aboard a pirate ship. We all be equal. And we'll share the spoils equally, too."

Nick and Willy smiled happily and nodded their agreement.

"Well then, I reckon ya got yourself a crew, Captain," Nick said. "Now, where's your ship?"

"That's the only hitch," Horacio snickered and puffed out his chest when the cowboy referred to his rank. "We have yet to acquire our vessel. I've got my eye on a Dutch ship that is anchored in the harbor. It has twenty cannons and room to build more gunports for added firepower. It's a small, sleek craft with little draft. So, she can maneuver in shallow water better than a heavy Spanish battleship. Sometimes a big ship is a disadvantage."

"And how do you know so much about ships?" Nick asked. "Are you really a captain?"

Horacio stammered. Then he hemmed and hawed for a moment before he said, "I may not have had my own ship, but I've studied the man-of-war I served aboard. I even had the pilot show me how to navigate. Being a quick learner and all, I had no difficulty figuring it out. I lost an eye and leg in a battle with a pirate ship. So, I have experienced war up close. If any of you are better schooled, I'm willing to reconsider. If not, I'm as much of a captain as you're gonna get."

"It don't look like you faired too well so far for a young fella," Willy observed.

"You mean this?" Horacio asked as he lifted his leg to show his peg. "If you look at the end, you can see the surprise I have for those who displease me."

When the two men looked at the end of his pegleg, they both saw the barrel of a sawed-off flintlock rifle sticking out of the end.

"Sometimes, a bit of bad luck can create an unforeseen advantage," Horacio said as he chuckled. "And it gave me three months resting up to study everything there was to know about sailing ships. I was a powder monkey during my time aboard the *HMS Hue*, so I'm well versed in cannon, too."

ten
the black widow

The Caribbean Sea

THE SMALL DUTCH cargo ship sat quietly, moored at the dock in the British port. Its captain was standing on the pier as the two-masted vessel was loaded with cargo, provisions, and ammunition. She bore twenty cannons to protect her valuables and was destined to sail to Europe via the Spanish Canary Islands, which were off the western coast of Central Africa.

The *Black Widow* would sail more than one thousand nautical miles to Port Rosario, located on the Spanish-owned island of Fuerteventura. Once there, she was to have a secret rendezvous with an English spy and eventually would set sail for the British Isles.

Her cargo was largely unknown, but rumors indicated the captain would transport anything and everything if the price were right. Captain Chase Ghast was well known for his ruthless methods and thieving nature. The British government secretly owned the

Black Widow, but she presently was sailing under a Dutch flag, all bits of information Horacio culled from the gossip in the saloons, bars, and taverns that dotted the seaport.

The more Horacio discovered about Captain Ghast, the less guilt he felt about his plan to steal the ship. Nobody had a good word for him. He was on the verge of becoming a pirate himself. He put money and power before anything else, including the wellbeing of his crew.

For Horacio, the *Black Widow* was the perfect prize. She was sleek, fast, and light when compared to most warships and other bearers of heavy cargo. A vessel with less draft could run closer to the coast in shallow water and go places where the larger ships could not. This made it the perfect choice for chasing down heavily laden cargo vessels. It also could outmaneuver or outrun most warships—American, Spanish, French, or British. Finally, its twin masts made it possible for a skeleton crew to operate.

Horacio realized most of the men he enlisted had little knowledge of ship navigation, but he was determined to make his dreams come true. So Hammer set his plan into motion.

He immediately began teaching his young sailors the ways of navigating the ocean's waters. In three days, the new crew of the *Black Widow* would take over the ship, remove the current crewmembers, and sail off into the night. Baring bad weather, he hoped to navigate to another island, one not too far away.

The ten orphans found a place to gather deep in the

jungle of Barbados. They had taken to the land, the climate and the plentiful amounts of food available for the picking. Willy's pockets always were stuffed with mangos, bananas and berries, among other things.

At first, they thought their hideout was a cave. But after extensive exploration, they discovered it was a passageway to a clearing with a crystal-clear freshwater spring. Fish could be seen swimming in its depths. Tadpoles darted about the shallows, and dragonflies bounced across the still water. Cattails poked out at its shoreline and swayed in the breeze.

The occasional trout would break the surface and devour insects and send ripples across the surface. Nobody could see their fire or hear their discussions. It was time to make their plan.

Horacio sat next to Nick and gazed into the eyes of the other eight members of the crew. Nobody said a word. It was if all were afraid to break the silence because it could trumpet bad luck.

"Today is Tuesday. I figure by Friday, we must be ready," Horacio said. "Our greatest problem will be finding a way to disable the crew. If we could find some way to poison their food, they would be unable to mount a resistance."

"Are you going to poison them all?" Aldo Rey asked, somewhat aghast. "I don't want any part of murder. Not like that. It's one thing to fight to defend yourself but I won't be part of murdering forty or fifty men."

"Of course, we're not going to murder anybody," Horacio replied sarcastically. "We just need to get them sick enough they can't resist. Does anybody know of anything that would make them ill but not kill them? I want them to be able to recover in a couple of days."

"I've heard holly berries will make you vomit and give you diarrhea something terrible," Jack Fury said. "Maybe we could slip some into their food."

"I have an idea," Celestia said. "I've been by the ship ten times in the last days, and every other night they have a dozen chickens delivered for supper. All we have to do is mix the holly berries in with the chicken feed and get them to eat it. By their cook's own hand, they all should be too sick to work or even walk on their own by midnight."

Horacio had instructed Celestia to pass by the ship several times a day to observe when the officers came and went. Dressed in man's clothing, she resembled a small boy. Hammer wanted to know when the crew took its meals, how many men usually manned the deck and any changes in the ship's daily routines.

Fox quickly became an integral part of the team and felt a special bond with the rest of the orphans—especially Willy Words, whose wisdom at such a young age drew her to him. But she had her secrets, too. Both Horacio and Nick scared her some. She knew neither would harm her and both would protect her with their lives. Rough and rugged, they were drawn to danger and adventure like moths to a campfire. Their thirst for the unknown seemed insatiable.

Celestia also understood Horacio up to a point. He was British after all, and she had known English people all her life. They generally thought themselves to be better than the lowly Irish. Putting that aside, she found herself developing a fondness for him. It was a similar feeling she held for Nick, but somehow different.

Nick's love of danger was raw and evident because he came from so far away. She found everything about him different and exciting, especially that casual drawl she heard when he spoke and the growl he made when he was angry.

Of the two, Nick scared her the most. Nonetheless, she was drawn to the more dangerous of the partners, possibly due to the fact she never knew what he was going to do as they faced the unknown. The Texan also accepted life with a confidence and boldness she had never seen in another man, often thumbing his nose at danger and authority, alike.

In the last two days, she reported the *Black Widow* was taking on provisions and preparing to sail soon. On most nights, just after their supper, half of the crew would wander into the city to enjoy all the varied sources of entertainment provided for sailors in the lively port.

She also knew when their food stock was delivered for their evening meal and what time they ate. The crew knew once it was at sea, fried chicken or freshly butchered meat would not see their plates for some time. After one day's delivery, Celestia followed the farmer back to his farm. She and Willy returned the next day to feed the farmer's chickens the holly berries. Then they waited.

As darkness fell across the island city, the nine

friends followed Hammer toward the ship. They moved from one shadow to another in groups of two until they were all assembled behind a shed that stood in the shadow of the *Black Widow*. It was around midnight when they heard the first of the men retch over the side of the gunwale. Another two followed. Then another five or more heaved.

Their plan was working, and the ship's gunwales were lined with some twenty men, all spewing tainted meals. The sound and smell of sickness assaulted the noses of the opportunistic gang of ten. The crew was spewing poison from both ends as foul aromas assaulted the air they breathed making their noses wrinkle up in distaste.

They waited for another hour to make sure all of the sailors had succumbed to the poison berries.

When Horacio and Nick led their buddies aboard, nobody was able to deny them access. The *Black Widow's* crew lay scattered across the main deck. They no longer made it to the gunwales to get sick; they heaved where they lay. The mess on the deck was horrendous, but the ruse had worked perfectly.

Soon, Donk was picking up one crewmember after another and tossing them overboard into the harbor. Nick kept a close eye on them to make sure they didn't drown. All seemed to have enough energy to dog paddle to safety.

"Quick now, climb those masts!" Horacio ordered as he planned a quick getaway. "Wishbone and Hambone, get down here and cast off the mooring lines and let's get underway before the sick sailors can raise the alarm."

In the previous days, Horacio had taken his crew, two men at a time, to observe the ship from a distance. He made several trips with different pairs of men and explained precisely what he wanted them to do when it came time to board and seize the *Black Widow*. Now, they nimbly climbed up the webbing to the masts and began to get the vessel underway. The wind was light, but the direction was good for a quick escape. They doused the running lights and sailed away into the darkness. The creaking wood of the hull was the only sound on a still night as the ship rolled and sliced nicely through the warm waters of the Caribbean Sea.

As expected, there was a considerable amount of confusion among the small crew due to their lack of experience. Between Horacio and Jack Fury, they were guided through their new duties. Lucky for them, the sea was calm with just enough breeze to push them along.

Horacio went below to the pilot's quarters, where navigation charts were stored. He brought what he needed to the deck and began setting a dead-reckoning course for the island of Tortuga. Hellsworth had heard it was a place where pirates were welcome, and he might find the rest of the crew he required to live out his dream. He had no idea, though, how he would go about enlisting men of such reckless blood.

eleven
tortuga

Tortuga - Caribbean Sea

THE FIRST RECORDED landing on Tortuga was by Christopher Columbus in 1492. Columbus was, on his way to discover what he thought would be India, but it turned out to be the Americas. During the golden years of piracy—the 1600s and 1700s—the island as often as not was controlled by buccaneers. Little had changed in the early years of the 1800s. Even though the island was claimed for the Queen of Spain, at times, it was still a stronghold for the outlaws of the sea.

All pirates needed somewhere to sell their valuable loot and cargo. There always were one or two corrupt island officials ready to line their pockets with profits from the sea's spoils. Greed motivated them to look the other way and never ask from where the valuables came.

Nick recalled how the five-cent novels he read as a youth portrayed pirates. They frequently captured ships with vast amounts of gold and silver bullion, valuable jewelry, and precious stones. Truthfully, most of the cargo pirates stole was everyday trade items that had to be bartered and stored in large warehouses. Then, the goods were resold to buyers across the islands and the continent. It was rare for a pirate to find a vessel laden with silver or gold.

The first pirates to arrive on the rocky island of Tortuga transformed it into a base for groups of adventurers, outlaws and thieves. Sailors, mutineers, marooners and escaped slaves lived free under the pirate flag. From their stronghold, they conducted raids on any ships they found in their waters and beyond. At the very beginning, the pirates on the colony of Tortuga were Frenchmen from neighboring Hispaniola or Haiti.

They adopted the name *boucaner* (butcher and meat curer) from the French. The word instilled fear in seafaring captains for the next two hundred years. When Jean le Vasseur, a one-time pirate and French military engineer, built a 24-gun fortress—called Fort de Rocher—to safeguard the island in 1630, warring vessels steered clear of the pirate's secret fortress.

Tortuga boasted pirates from as far away as Holland, England, and Portugal. As the island's population of cutthroats increased, they struggled to organize themselves, creating a loose fraternity, known as the *Brethren of the Coast*. Often the same pirates received privateer commissions from France or England, a thorn in Spain's naval pride. As a result, the Spanish launched several unsuccessful attacks on the island. After Jean le Vasseur, the English pirate Sir

Henry Morgan arrived. He was known across the globe for his assaults on the Spanish Armada.

As Spain's hold on South America weakened, its ability to maintain power across the vast seas waned, too. Eventually, Spain would surrender the countries and islands of the Caribbean. By 1823, the heyday of Tortuga was long past, although there was still a presence of pirates on the island. With their numbers diminished, the island's future was bleak.

Of course, Horacio already had heard tales of Tortuga during his time on the British man-of-war. So, he believed his crew could find a safe haven there and procure more hands. It made sense that a town run by pirates would have sailors looking for jobs. It remained to be seen if Horacio and Nick could garner the trust needed to survive a layover on the island.

They also had a vessel of stolen cargo to sell. Although there were other places throughout the Caribbean to do business, Tortuga was the only place Horacio trusted, based on his reliable sources.

When Captain Hellsworth and First Mate Risk stood at the massive helm and steered the *Black Widow* into Tortuga harbor; rowboats came out to meet them. A sizable torch burned brightly from the bow of each of the boats. They released an aroma of coconut oil and plums of black smoke. Upon their approach, Horacio had raised a black flag to signify their pirate identity.

The flag, made by Willy and Celestia, was void of any emblem, but signaled their friendly intent to the well-armed island. The fort, with its 24-cannon, stood out in the foreground. The entire crew knew if they made a wrong move, hell would rain down on the *Black Widow*.

As the ship gathered sails and slowed to a crawl, the boats escorted it to anchorage. Jack Fury barked orders to the crew to weigh anchor and prepare to be boarded.

Rope webbing was lowered from the side of the gunwales to give dangerous looking men access to the *Black Widow's* deck. They wore brightly colored clothes and sour faces. Nick immediately reached for his pistols, but Horacio stopped him with a warning look.

"Now wouldn't be a good time to challenge our hosts," Horacio whispered. Then, he smiled as the first pirates stepped on board.

The orphans were silent, but the men boarding the vessel quickly noticed the small crew of ten. They were young but each was armed with a rifle or pistol, weapons they had found on the cargo ship when they confiscated her.

Donk was the only man who didn't brandish a gun. Instead, he held heavy sledgehammers in each of his paws. His eyes narrowed and his brow furrowed. Of the ten, he loomed as the most menacing.

The last individual to board the *Black Widow* was an older man of maybe sixty years. He wore all black, even his shirt and scarf. But he greeted the newcomers with a cheerful face and seemed far less threatening.

"Hello, gentlemen," the polite pirate said. "I'm Captain Boris Blade and I am the governor of Tortuga. You people do realize where you are, don't you?"

"I am Captain Horacio Hellsworth, and this is First

Mate Nick Risk," the Hammer said. "I know for a fact our lot be in Cayona of Tortuga. We may be young, but we are not ignorant, sir."

"You seem to be short on crewmembers, Captain," Blade said. "And all so young."

"We're old enough to know how to use these," Nick growled and patted his pistols. Horacio shot him another stern look.

"Excuse my friend," Horacio implored. "He's from Texas. It takes him a little while to become accustomed to strangers. They say the part of America he hails from is hard country. Rest assured, we come here to sell our cargo and have no other intentions. We may spend a spell in Cayona while we outfit our ship properly. That is, if it is with your approval, Captain Blade."

When Boris Blade heard mention of business, he became even nicer and said, "Only a true outlaw would have the gall to sail into Tortuga flying a black flag. Welcome to our island, gentlemen. Even you, Mr. Texas. No one will bother you here. We have a code among us pirates and it is written in stone. I am sure even your American friend will find the people here friendly and the ladies accommodating."

"Why, thank you, sir," Horacio said as he tipped his hat.

Nick looked sideways at Horacio and frowned. Then he tipped his hat as well.

Finally, Captain Blade pointed to the fort's 24 cannon and said with a wicked smile, "They guarantee everyone behaves themselves."

twelve
island life

The Island of Tortuga

CAPTAIN BLADE WAS A SHREWD BUSINESSMAN, who could smell revenue in a pile of dung. So, when the *Black Widow* and her crew of one young woman and nine men arrived at his island, he saw profits. Where some might have perceived danger, he saw an opportunity to boost his own ranks with new, young conscriptions. New blood often was accompanied by uncommon rewards to be traded with merchants. He also recognized the captain and his young crew hungered for the pirate way of life.

"Perhaps my island again will become the center of the pirate world with the help of the *Black Widow*," Captain Blade whispered to himself.

Blade had been overseeing Cayona for more than a decade and had watched its population dwindle. Too many crews set sail but never returned. Inevitably, some ships were sunk, and their crews captured. Others simply abandoned the lifestyle and sailed off in search of new beginnings.

So, Tortuga had fallen on hard times. A boost in trade and personnel was direly needed. Captain Blade turned on the charm and greeted the newcomers with open arms.

Their good fortune buoyed the confidence of the young crew. Under different circumstances, the *Black Widow* may have been greeted by the fort's cannons, boarded and robbed. The island had protected its own for two centuries and remained a place where pirate captains could get top price for their goods and feel safe and secure.

Horacio and Nick's crew were as pleased with the outcome as possible. All feared they would hang from yardarms for stealing the Dutch vessel. Lo-and-behold, Horacio had guided them to a safe harbor and they even had money in their pockets. Most importantly, the colony of rejects accepted the orphan crew warmly.

Late at night, the original group of ten sat around the captain's quarters of the *Black Widow*. The scent of coconut oil lingered in the cabin as four lamps teetered with the gentle roll of the ship. The orange glow reflected on the faces of the eager adventurers. The creaking wood from the heavy hull was the only sound as the crew waited for Horacio and Nick to preside over the meeting.

"How is the work going on the gun ports?" Horacio asked.

"We've made enough new slots to install twenty more cannons," Willy replied. "We've purchased ten artillery units from Captain Blade, so we will have to find another ten before it's completed."

"That leaves the saloon as our last project," Nick said as he began to chuckle. "It'll be just like back home."

"Do you really think the local pirates will choose an American-style western saloon over their rum taverns?" Celestia asked with a raised brow.

"Why, of course, they will. They'll like it just fine," Nick said and grinned. "There's only a couple of places in town to get a drink, and they are identical. I reckon everybody likes something new and different. And it will give us a place to stay other than the *Black Widow*. I like it here in town. All I need is a little bit of Texas to make it feel like home."

"What we need to do is open our own warehouse," Horacio said. "That would maximize our profits."

"What? That would create competition for Captain Blade?" Skinny interjected. "Remember, he's been more than fair to us."

"He's treated us well because he saw a profit," Nick grumbled. "I don't trust him a lick. I never did, and I never will."

"Just the same, I believe we should focus on what we have to do today and not what we might do months from now," Celestia said. "Look where we've come from and where we are now. Would any of you have believed we could enjoy such freedom? We have a ship of our own and we live in a community where we are welcome. None of us are indentured or working at the will of the rich, like Hambone and Wishbone once did. I once faced a much darker future; I can assure you."

"She's as right as rain," Jack Fury said and added a warning. "Greed is the curse of many. Now, who would have thought we would ever have our own ship? I choose to applaud our good fortunate. By all rights, we all could have been hanged."

"Until Texas Nick saved us, we had no future at all," Wishbone said. "My brother and me were born into slavery. We never dreamed of freedom until you boys came along. For us, this has been a miracle. Before now we didn't even know what the word *free* meant. It'd be a shame to ruin it, now wouldn't it?"

"Maybe you're right," Horacio said as he pondered on Wishbone's words. "We have plenty of time. Who knows what will happen a year from now?"

"I figure we best not lose sight of our original objectives," Nick said. "Getting the ship fitted out to capture cargo vessels is first. My saloon is secondary. Beyond that, I'm not much interested in anything else."

Horacio was as ambitious as a captain could be, but he never disrespected his crew of friends. He always listened to reason, which was more than could be said for most of the captains who worked out of Tortuga. The orphans had a bond unlike others. Nowhere else could ex-slaves like Hambone and Wishbone work alongside an outlaw like Skinny, a scallywag like Donk and a female as smart as Celestia.

One and all of the orphans had been given a second chance at life. Perhaps it was not the path most would have chosen, but it was the only path open for them. It was either choose a future with hope or do nothing and die at the hands of violent men who do bad things to wayward teens.

All had a good reason to hold grudges. Some, like Nick and Horacio, did. They had suffered so much in their lives; their souls were permanently scarred. As captain and first mate discussed their future, the others sat cross-legged on the *Black Widow's* deck and gave the two leaders their undivided attention.

"What we have to do quickly is secure the rest of our crew," Horacio said. "We need another thirty men just to be able to man all the cannon, not to mention to tend to the sails. It's a big job, especially when we make our first attempt at boarding another vessel."

"I've been talking to some of the other sailors in town," Nick replied as he chewed on a tobacco plug. "Most of them are older, but many of 'em ain't happy with their captains. They never go out in search of ships to raid anymore. I could get twenty men together in a single day. I swear, there's a lot of bored pirates on this island. Before we got here, things were just about to shrivel up and blow away. That's why Captain Blade was so happy to see us. If not for an injection of fresh blood, most of the men would have already abandoned the town or died from natural causes. Yeah, I reckon our arrival was a godsend."

"Who are the men you picked?" Skinny asked. "Some of those older pirates be mean as rattlesnakes."

"Out of the hundred or so pirates that live here, only about half of them work anymore," Horacio explained. "Most of the captains are over sixty. So, those are the crewmen we need to interview. Some will remain loyal to their leaders, but there are still a good number who have the fever for gold and silver. Like their leaders, they seek fortunes so one day they can lie back and live fat off the land."

"From now on, each of us must enlist recruits," Nick said as his eyes moved across the faces of his friends. "As soon as we get the cannons installed and we get some practice with a new crew, we'll be good to go."

It didn't take but a week to find enough men to man the *Black Widow*. Each of the recruits were experienced pirates. All looked up to Captain Hellsworth and First Mate Risk. When the men boarded the ship for their first practice run, Hammer saw hunger in their eyes. The promise of plundering a cargo vessel, chock-full of valuables, made their hearts race.

Many of the men hadn't been to sea for months. It had been more than a year since most had boarded a rival vessel with deadly intent. All of the crew, new and old, looked happily toward future adventures.

No one missed the hard look in the eyes of their new taskmasters, though. The captain and his first mate already had growing reputations of cunning bravery and strong leadership. Nick Risk was admired for his skills with his wheel-guns. And Horacio for his bold behavior even though he was missing a leg and an eye.

As soon as they lost sight of land, Horacio and Nick studied the navigation charts and mapped out a route with favorable winds. Winds would provide the speed for the maneuvers they needed to practice in order to later overtake and capture cargo ships.

Skinny sat high above the deck in the crow's nest and watched the horizon through a long spyglass. He combed the sea for enemy vessels or unsuspecting cargo ships, but spotted nothing but water for as far as the eye could see.

Nick had grown to love the smell of salt in the air as the versatile ship sliced easily through the warm water of the Caribbean. As they tacked along with the wind, they practiced manning the forty cannons strung along the gunports on either side of the ship. Wishbone and Hambone were in charge of keeping the powder and cannonballs supplied to each of the weapons.

By the time they sailed back to Tortuga, all operations worked like a fine Swiss watch. The most agile of the crew were the Bone Brothers, the nickname the new sailors fashioned for the two black mates. With regular meals and plenty of exercise, their cord-like muscles rippled up and down their arms and backs. For them, life could not be better. No matter what the outcome, they had absolutely no regrets.

Even Celestia had changed since she landed on the island. She discarded her men's clothing and adapted to her own style of dress. She wore fencing pants for comfort and tact. A white shirt covered her blossoming breasts, and her thin waist was accented with a wide belt from where a short sword hung. She garnered respect and accepted nothing less. She wore one of Nick Risk's old straw cowboy hats over her long blond hair and had a brace of flintlock pistols shoved into her wide belt.

Celestia and Willy seemed to have created a bond

over the months since their escape. Even though the Atlantic Ocean separated their homelands, they interacted like brother and sister. Willy was smart, and Celestia soaked in every word.

Jack Fury and Aldo Rey were drawn together as the Cornishman's family had long ago owned a home near the Spanish border with Portugal. They shared great interests in food and wine.

When the *Black Widow* silently glided into the port, Nick jumped down from the towering gunwales and onto the dock, his boots hammering the timber. When he looked up, Horacio was smiling down on him with a twinkling eye. He anxiously awaited the gangplank so he could disembark with his teak pegleg. He looked up at the sun, adjusted the black patch over his right eye and moved from the bridge to land with amazing speed and grace. Aboard the *Black Widow*, a person hardly noticed he was disabled. Only on land did his wounds seem to hinder him.

When his peg hit the deck, he proffered his hand to his partner with a grin. They had done it. They had secured a ship and an experienced crew. Nick even had a Texas-style saloon in the middle of Cayona. Life was indeed good.

thirteen
the texas saloon

The island of Tortuga

JUST LIKE NICK HAD PREDICTED, the Texas Saloon was a total success. The men who they called pirates were pretty much like everybody else in the world. Men and women from distant lands, shared a love of entertainment, good food and drink.

Of course, not everybody that lived on the island was a pirate. Some men and women worked for the town's businesses. Captain Blade acted more like a governor than the leader of buccaneers.

To make the saloon more interesting, Nick had placed a shooting range and horseshoe pits along the long building's right side. The first night the Texas Saloon opened, the place was swamped with curious and adventurous customers. Risk even organized a long-rifle shooting contest and a quick-draw competition.

Celestia took command of Skinny and Aldo behind the bar as the mob stood ten deep waiting for a drink. Luckily, Aldo spoke fluent Spanish, Portuguese, and French. So, every customer was adequately greeted. Nick strutted around the place as proud owner, even though it was only partly his. He sported a brace of new four-shot single-action Collier wheel-guns. Light from the saloon's numerous lanterns glinted from the shiny nickel plating of his new pistols.

On the other side of the building, a pig and a steer were roasting on massive spits. Hot orange coals illuminated the evening, which made the cooks' faces glow orange. The smell of cooking meat filled the air as Dunk turned the massive handle of the spit. A gentle island breeze carried the smoke off into the night as the meat sizzled and dripped hot fat.

When it came time for the shooting contest, most of the men—and a few women—stood in a long line to sign up. Nick had promised the winner of the event a brand-new Collier revolver, identical to the ones he carried, which he had shipped from overseas from the very man who invented them.

Nick officiated at what he called *"The Shootout."* He wanted his saloon to feel as much like home as it possibly could. He even covered the barroom floor with sawdust. Brass spittoons were scattered throughout. Large mirrors ran the entire length of the bar, making the room look even larger than it was.

Over fifty men had signed up for the shooting contest and it took some time to dwindle the numbers down to the finalists. All the while, Texas Nick's lips formed an amused grin. Most of the shooters used cap-and-ball weapons, and some were quite proficient. Among the ragtag bunch were men who had served aboard French, Spanish, English and Portuguese ships.

The Texan felt it wouldn't be fair if the owner participated. In the probable case he won, there could be discontent among the competitors. Instead, he planned to give the crowd a show of sorts, an exhibition of his skills.

Once the shootout was concluded, Nick dazzled everyone with his quick-draw abilities. When he shot off eight rounds without reloading his revolvers, the audience was left in awe, especially as every bullet embedded in the bullseye.

Onlookers were convinced he would have won the contest had he participated and pleased as pudding he didn't. The host had shown his good manners in allowing another to win. He handed over his own Collier revolver to the victor, a personal gift from Texas Nick Risk.

When Captain Blade walked into the saloon, everybody immediately sensed his arrival. The room quietened noticeably, and many turned their heads to look toward the man who had made all this possible. Of course, his entrance didn't go unnoticed by Nick or Horacio.

Nick had always made it clear he didn't trust the so-called governor. Over the months, Blade had given them a fair shake, one that was to his benefit as well as the newcomers. Nick changed his opinion. He not only shared respect for Blade, but he won the hearts and loyalties of most of the island's sailors. It made recruiting crewmen to man the sails and cannon an easy task.

Most of the island's inhabitants were over forty. So, the young crew had done more than recharge the community with hope; they provided the best promise of new cargoes of significant value.

When valuable booty was seized, everyone on the island benefited—from those who worked in the warehouses to the pirates themselves.

"Come on in, Captain," Nick called over the raucous crowd. "Have a drink of American whiskey with us. It'll put some starch in your socks."

Horacio had to chuckle at Nick's attitude. He was as good a friend as he had ever had, even though they were both as different as black and white.

Hammer adjusted the patch over his right eye and said, "Join us, sir. The whiskey is different than that of the Scottish or Irish, but I must admit it is an acquired taste I have come to admire."

Celestia smiled as she placed three glasses on the bar, brought out an unopened bottle of Jim Beam bourbon and pulled the cork. She poured three fingers into each glass and flashed her white teeth at the trio. The crowd went back to its business and the noise in the room again rose.

"Cheers, gentlemen," Captain Blade said as he raised his American whiskey in a toast. He grimaced as he tasted the dark liquid and added, "It looks like you're having quite a success."

Nick grinned like a possum and said, "Thank ya, Chief. I figured you'd come around and we'd get along in the end."

fourteen
the duel

The Texas Saloon—Tortuga

SOME TORTUGA CITIZENS believed the roots of the challenge came from the shooting match on the day the Texas Saloon opened. Others said the Frenchman simply hated Americans, especially extraordinarily bold Texans like Nick Risk, Willy Words, and Skinny Razor.

The challenge didn't come about in the heat of the moment. Most Texas gunfights were brought on by a combination of too much whiskey and a room full of guns. Of course, a general lack of law in Texas in the early 1800s contributed, too.

Nick, Skinny, and Willy spent many of their days in the Texas Saloon. The midday summer heat in the tropics matched the hottest summer days in Texas. However, the mosquitoes were fierce and as big as small dragonflies. Their constant buzzing was almost as much a nuisance as their bites.

The boys had pulled up to three empty chairs at a

six-man poker table. Cash and coin lay stacked on the wooden top as the dealer skillfully dealt hands. He pulled one card at a time from the deck and, with a barely noticeable flick of his wrist, sent the cards spiraling across the table. Each card stopped in front of the appropriate player.

They were deep into the game when the room quieted as a group of Frenchmen entered. They were easily recognized by their fancy frocks and frilly shirts. They wore tri-cornered hats over curly wigs.

Everyone took note the French pirates were armed for war. All but Jean L'Escuyer II. He strode across the room with an air that only the French aristocracy possessed. He was dressed identically but wore a pair of exquisite gray pigskin gloves.

The stack of money being wagered at the poker table, prevented its players from noticing the Frenchmen's approach. All eyes were affixed on the cards lying face down before them and the pile of silver and gold coin stacked high on the middle. The stakes in the game had become steep, and each player was looking for the telltale sign of a bluff or a small hint of glee for a good hand.

"Are you First Mate Nickolas Risk?" Captain L'Escuyer demanded with an air of superiority.

Nick didn't like having his poker game interrupted, especially when much of the pot's money was his. He had no intention of losing it.

Nick gritted his teeth as he swung his head toward the Frenchman and said, "Can't you see we're in the middle of a game, fool?"

The retaliation from Jean L'Escuyer was immediate as he pulled off one of his elegant gloves and slapped Nick across the left cheek.

"I challenge you to a duel, sir," the Frenchman spat. "This afternoon at eighteen hundred hours sharp."

Nick was initially taken off guard. Never in his adult life had a man acted toward him in such a disrespectful manner. He quickly was spurned to anger, and his hands went for his four-shot Collier wheel gun.

The four pirates who accompanied the French captain foresaw the cowboy's reaction and already had their flintlock pistols aimed at Risk before he could defend himself.

"You're being mighty bold coming into my place of business all aggressive like," Nick said.

"This is how civilized people settle their differences on the continent," the captain arrogantly replied. "As I have proposed the challenge, sir, you may choose the weapons. Would you like pistols or swords?"

"I thought you said it was my choice," Nick replied as a grin spread across his face. "I choose knives."

The French captain was so surprised, he stood with his mouth open for a moment as his bodyguards looked on questioningly.

"Well, ya said it was my choice, didn't ya, Chief?" Nick said. "Or have you turned yeller all of a sudden?"

You could see the captain seethe over the American's words and his choice of the crudest weapons. Finally, he broke the silence and said, "Will my daggers be acceptable?"

"It's fine with me," Nick said as he grumbled and

slowly reached behind his back. The French body-guards reacted defensively as Nick added, "Take it easy now, boys. I was just getting my knife."

Nick's grin widened when he pulled an extremely large Bowie knife from the sheath he had in the back of his britches.

"Them's nothin' but pig stickers," Nick said as he laughed in the face of the man who intended to kill him. "Now here's a knife, sparky."

The big blade sparkled in the lamplight as Nick moved it before him like he was playing with the French captain. Then he grabbed it in his fist, blade down, and drove it deep into the top of the timber table.

* * *

By six o'clock that afternoon, most people in Cayona had heard how the Frenchman had challenged the Texan. The duel's location was on the beach at the water's edge. A circle was drawn in the sand and a straight line divided the circle in two. The knife fight was to be held within the boundaries of the ring. If one of the opponents stepped outside, he would be consid-ered a coward and run off the island. As in all duels, whether with sword or pistol, death would determine the loser.

The cosmopolitan crowd chattered with excitement in a half dozen languages. Eyes sparkled wide with trepi-dation, and a constant murmur ebbed and flowed through the waiting mass of townsfolk.

A few vendors had gotten wind of the event and were selling their magic soap, canned fruit, and glass bottles of mystery elixirs to onlookers.

The Frenchman arrived first in a fine carriage, driven by two white horses. When the driver jumped down and opened the door, the famous pirate stepped down and allowed his evil eyes to peruse the crowd of spectators.

He wore a silvery wig with curly locks of hair, giving him the look of an aristocrat. He was a short man with a quick temper, intelligent eyes and an apparent total disregard for danger. He was not so different in that regard as other men of the same trade.

A goatee grew from his chin, waxed to a neat point, as were the fine tips of his mustache. Although his second stood by his side with a highly polished maple box cradled in his arms, he carried no visible weapons.

It was two minutes to six when three horses charged the beach with three men wearing cowboy hats. Each Texan pulled their horse to a sliding halt and slid out of their saddles. Texas Nick wore riding britches and American Indian moccasins. He was bare from the waist up. Muscles stood out on his arms and back like thick cords of rope. Sunlight glared off the layer of sweat that covered his skin. The muscles of his abs and pecs rippled as he moved toward the circle with a Bowie knife in each hand. He towered over the Frenchman.

The French captain's second announced the rules of the dual as each man stepped into the ring, but Nick paid him no heed. The rules were clear, and he saw no need to delay the inevitable. So, he crouched low to engage his enemy, his eyes no more than slits. Immediately, he lunged over the line and slashed his blades at Jean L'Escuyer. The pirate captain parried the assault but was taken off guard by the Texan's sudden aggression.

"I didn't come here to talk, sparky," Nick said. Then, he spat into the sand and added, "Let's dance."

Nick's friends were pressed as close as they could without interfering with the fight or putting themselves in danger. Willy, Skinny, Jack, and Donk kept their eyes on the crowd to ensure the fight was fair. They feared a Frenchman was in hiding, waiting to strike out and kill Nick when he defeated the pompous captain. Nerves made Skinny's eye twitch randomly as Willy bit on his lower lip. Celestia stood beside Donk with her hands bunched into fists and pressed against her chest. She was nervous and her breathing erratic.

The five French guards stood on the other side of the circle, but they were standing down in light of an honorable duel, even if it was somewhat unusual.

The sight of two men from different worlds dueling for honor turned the event into a spectacle. Nick was a man from a hard land, where violence was a daily way of life. The French captain was from the city of Marseille and was accustomed to formality. Today, he had mixed feelings about what he had created.

His anger boiled the day he was so easily defeated by one of the newcomers in the long-rifle shooting contest. He became even more infuriated by the showboating by Risk and his fancy work with his revolver.

He sought to prove he was a better shot with a pistol, especially in a duel. Men didn't shoot as straight when another was shooting back. Instead, the American turned the tables on him. He now was forced to prove himself with a familiar weapon, but one of which he was not a master.

Daggers were part of an officer's arsenal, along with his sword and pistol. He had trained his whole life with both the sword and dagger, and his skill was commendable. But now, he stood before a man who had no fear of danger or his opponent. It was a fact that shook him to his core.

Perhaps his uncontrollable need to seek revenge had made him act rashly. It was too late to back down, though. As a gentleman, he had to prove he was no coward; he had committed himself to a situation with only one honorable result. With each pass of the Texan's Bowie knives, the captain managed to parry. Try as he may, he could not achieve a dominant position. The American moved with catlike quickness. He would crouch low to make a pass, then roll and jump back to his feet.

On one such attack, L'Escuyer finally saw the opportunity for a counterattack. He lunged for Nick's side. With lightning quickness, Risk swung his right foot out and kicked the Frenchman's legs out from under him.

Nick swung his right knife at the captain's hand, which held a dagger. It was poised to drive the spiked weapon into Risk's heart when suddenly, the Frenchman screamed and raised his hand in the air.

Blood spurted from stubs. Four fingers and a dagger lay in the sand.

Nick backed away and dropped his hands to his sides, the knives still clenched in his fists. His desire for violence had passed; he had made his point. He realized he didn't have to kill the arrogant European; his wounds would end the Frenchman's dueling career.

"Hush up now! You'll wake the dead, fool," Nick shouted to the captain. Then he spat a foot-long stream of tobacco juice into the sand beside the squealing officer and happily departed.

fifteen
captain banshee

Cayona Harbor, Tortuga

HAMMER WAS NOT the only pirate captain sailing the high seas in the summer of 1823. Piracy had, in some way or another, existed since the first vessels began to cross the long stretches of water that covers two-thirds of the earth's surface. Even Julius Cesar was said to have been kidnapped by pirates.

Those who were lucky enough to retire in Tortuga thought piracy would never completely disappear. Active buccaneers, those who scoured the seas for plunder, felt the shadow of death chased them daily. Two men—Horacio "Hammer" Hellsworth and Zachary Banshee—battled for the right to be the most feared pirate captain of the Seven Seas.

Fear was a factor of paramount importance for seafaring men. Banshee intended to prevail in the face of the new competition.

The veteran pirate was a fat man who stood about

five feet eight. He resembled a little Napoleon and wore a fancy frock and vest. A silver chain ran from a button-hole, draped across his big belly and disappeared into his vest pocket. Fury and meanness resided in the black chunks of coal he had for eyes. A cruel frown never left his face and made most men uncomfortable.

Banshee once was an officer in the Queen's Royal Navy and had years of sailing and warfare experience. His body was covered with scars he wore as proud tattoos of battles won and lost. His dark hair and beard were so curly it gave him an unruly appearance.

The captain wore more medals on the breast of his black frock than Napoleon. They marked him as a captain of distinction, even though they were self-decorations. To top off the costume, he wore a black felt bicorne or two-corner hat. He made a habit of hiding one hand inside the flap of his fancy jacket. Unlike General Bonaparte, he didn't hold a cancer-ridden stomach. Banshee kept his hand hidden so he could dissimulate the small two-shot pistol he kept just inside his lapel.

Captain Zachery Banshee possessed none of the good qualities of Captain Hellsworth or Texas Nick. He was just as cruel a pirate as he had been a naval officer for Her Majesty's Royal Navy. The queen's captains all were selected for their brutal tenacity and were the most ruthless to sail the Seven Seas. Banshee often set his men loose on unsuspecting island villages, where they raped and pillaged the innocent inhabitants.

Like Hammer, he was a Londoner, but the similarities stopped there. He came from an aristocratic family and began to practice piracy with the blessing of the Queen of England. He found the lifestyle addictive and when the time came to relinquish his ship, he turned on his masters and kept the man-of-war. He used it to rob the very vessels he once was ordered to protect.

He possessed great insight into how the British Navy moved and acted against ships that flew the flags of its enemies. He knew every trick of the trade when it came to deceiving the targets he approached. As his vessel had initially been British, most ships would assume the obvious when he struck the English colors. This gave him time to approach his targets with little to no suspicion. A sea battle immediately would ensue when Banshee ran up the black flag. Most often it was too late for his targets to turn and run.

The *Gray Ghost* had just crossed the Atlantic Ocean via the Canary Islands and Brazil. It was sailing north to enter the Caribbean Sea via the northern coast of South America. Banshee had learned a Spanish fleet recently had sailed from Cadiz and was expected to weigh anchor in the coming weeks on the island of San Andres, Colombia. The captain could only assume this indicated they would be there to pick up a shipment of valuables.

Banshee believed he knew what routes the ships would take as there were only so many friendly ports for vessels to dock. Many islands were possessions of the American, French, English, or Spanish.

Spain had declared ownership over most of South America, along with Puerto Rico and Cuba. So, he was sure one of two islands would be the initial destination of the Spanish fleet. It would take time to restock supplies and make repairs before they made the last leg of the long journey back to the Canary Islands and eventually Europe.

He planned to find the location where they anchored for supplies. Then he would follow them at a distance before striking.

He was certain they would first stop in Cartagena to stock up on provisions for the long journey.

When the *Gray Ghost* sailed into the Cayona Harbor, she was flying the Jolly Roger. Most pirates used a simple black flag, but the more flamboyant captains opted for designs that warned of doom. Banshee chose a flag with two white bones crossed below a broken cranium on a black field.

As soon as the ship neared the port, a brass bell in the town square began to sound the official alarm that a vessel was approaching. Pirates and ordinary citizens rushed to the beach to see the massive warship drop anchor and prepare to come ashore.

As usual, Captain Blade was there to meet and greet all visitors, be they newcomers or old acquaintances like Captain Banshee. The island governor wasn't smiling as he did when Horacio, Nick, and their crew arrived. His expression was solemn, and his eyes darted about suspiciously at the shore party.

Blade walked right up to the visitor, tipped his hat, and said, "Captain Banshee, what brings you back to Tortuga?"

"Why, I am a pirate, aren't I?" Banshee replied with

an air of disrespect. "I have as much right to come here as the next buccaneer."

"Be forewarned," Captain Blade said in earnest. "The last time you were on the island, we had several killings. This time I don't expect a repeat of your crew's actions."

"Some of my men were killed, too," Banshee retorted with a sneer. "That's what we do for a living, is it not?"

"You know as well as I do the original charter declared any killing of a comrade is punishable by death," Captain Blade said. "If it weren't for our charter laws, the island would cease to be the haven it is."

By now, Risk and Hellsworth had walked up behind Blade, and they were listening intently to the conversation. The tall Texan was beginning to fume, but Horacio laid a hand on his forearm to ward off a confrontation. His first mate's short fuse had become legendary.

"This is not Texas, Nick," Horacio whispered to his tall friend.

Nick took a moment to calm the demons, breathed deeply and forced a smile. He bit his tongue for fear he might say what he was thinking. All his life, words had a habit of walking right out of his mouth before he could stop them, frequently offending the receiving party.

As Banshee and Blade dueled and parried with each other, Nick quickly grew impatient and left the beach.

Horacio followed because he wanted to keep an eye on his friend. He didn't want him to start a feud in Cayona. He decided it was best to let the island governor and the obnoxious Englishman sort out their differences.

Later that night, Horacio and Nick stood at the long timber bar in the Texas Saloon. It had been polished to a fine finish and bottles lined the wall behind it. They offered a wide selection of spirits, impressive considering where they were. As luck would have it, they had a vast array of alcohol and liquors plundered from ships from across the world.

A bottle of Jim Beam whiskey and two glasses of brown spirits sat in front of the pair of friends. Horacio sipped at his drink, but Nick lifted his to his lips and tossed it back in one gulp. It was another sign of how different the two were, yet how well they somehow complemented each other. Their skills were many and their loyalty without question.

They had been on Tortuga for many months—soon to be a year—and acquired the admiration of most of the island inhabitants. Every citizen knew who they were; they stood out wherever they went on the island. Even Celestia had become known across the rocky surface of Tortuga for her bold manner and striking beauty.

Most of the people who frequented the saloon had become friends of the owners since the day they arrived on the beach. Now, Banshee's return was the talk of the town. Some had known him in the past; others knew him by reputation. The captain's initial attitude made Nick and Horacio curious.

Horacio's thirst for education attracted him to Banshee, no matter what the risk. Hammer knew the brash captain had a lifetime of knowledge that was valuable. Nick viewed Banshee as a threat, and the Texan only knew one way to deal with such aggression—head-on. Had Horacio not stopped him that afternoon, Nick very well might have pulled down on Banshee, an offense that might have led to banishment from the island.

It was nearly midnight when the veteran pirate and three of his men finally found their way to the Texas Saloon. The bourbon bottle was almost empty, and Nick and the Hammer were standing at the bar discussing their future. As soon as the famous pirate entered the room, the hair on the back of Nick's neck stood on end and goose bumps stampeded up and down his arms. He felt his heart hammer between his temples as his anger suddenly soared.

Banshee's companions were all stout men, like their captain. Each crewmember had two flintlock pistols and a pair of knives shoved into their belts. All four were intoxicated; Nick and Horacio were into their cups as well.

Horacio found their new guest's arrival no more than an inconvenience, but Nick viewed it as a deliberate threat, maybe as much as a challenge. So, the Texan's nerves tensed as the drunken captain stepped their way.

"Well, what have we here?" Captain Banshee slurred. "What do you two lads think you're doing on this island? Why you're no more than a couple of pups."

Nick's eyes shot hot daggers at the scoundrel, but he held his tongue and his temper.

Horacio simply smiled and said, "I'll take that to be unoffensive, but it's only due to my gentle nature. I must warn you, though, my partner here is not such a forgiving soul. You know how Americans can be. So, if you would be so kind, refrain from offensive insinuations while you are present in our establishment. It would be much appreciated. You understand it is in everyone's best interest to avoid any unpleasant situations."

Captain Banshee squinted one eye, raised an eyebrow and frowned. He sighed, shook his head and tried to tamper his anger over the audacity of the young captain.

Of course, Banshee already had heard a great deal about the unlikely pirates. He had heard tell of their exploits in several ports before arriving on Tortuga. He considered their cunning theft of the *Black Widow* a remarkable achievement.

In fact, the aging and overweight captain of the *Gray Ghost* was jealous, resentful of their youth and success. The fame they had acquired at such an early age was at his expense. The exploits of Captain Zachery Banshee no longer were revered. It was the young pups and their crew of misfits who were the talk of the Seven Seas. Hellsworth's disrespectful greeting had him seething mad.

"You two may be able to outmaneuver a town of

aging pirates who no longer sail the seas anymore, but not men such as us," Captain Banshee scolded, sounding more like a threat than a statement. "Careful now, or you'll find you've bitten off more than you can chew."

Nick's mouth turned into a hard line as he gritted his teeth and poured two more fingers of whiskey into his glass. He tossed it back and growled. When he turned his eyes to the men who stood behind Banshee, as they all three reached for their pistols.

As Horacio and Banshee stared each other down, neither of the captains were aware of what was happening around them. Nick, however, missed nothing. He read tension in their muscles as they gripped the handles of their guns.

It happened so fast, onlookers said they didn't even see Nick pull his pistols. Both of his four-shot wheel-guns barked and flashed fire in the blink of an eye. Six bullets spat out of the Texan's guns as two skillfully placed holes appeared in the chests of Banshee's crewmen. Gunsmoke immediately clouded the room.

The captains were so taken aback by the sudden action, neither had time to react. Nick swung his revolver toward the head of Captain Banshee, and he pulled back the hammer one last time.

"I got a couple of bullets left just for you, sparky," Nick growled with hate in his eyes.

Banshee wasn't stupid enough to go for his guns with the Texan holding such an advantage. He knew he would be dead before his hand touched the wooden handle of his sidearm.

"Who in the hell do you think you are?" the captain demanded as his eyes looked for life in the three dead men on the floor.

"I'm the man who shot three of your crew before they could blink, so I should warn you that you are standing on shaky ground," Nick said in just over a whisper.

"Being as this saloon is ours, I must insist you leave at once," Horacio said, visibly shocked at the quick temper of his partner. "If not, I doubt your fate will be any different than that of your friends."

You could see the heavyset pirate captain struggle with his anger and pride. His usual behavior would be to attack at once, but he saw something different in the American. He didn't believe he could be bluffed.

The English captain's eyes passed from Nick to his men, who were bleeding out on the wood plank floor, and back at the Texan. His youthful face was impossible to read. His angry eyes told him the first mate wouldn't hesitate to shoot one more time. So, Banshee stood down and walked toward the double bat-wing doors. When he arrived at the exit, he turned and said, "This ain't over, you sons-of-bitches. Not by a long shot."

Nick lifted his arm and aimed his pistol at the man near the exit. Then, Banshee was gone.

The next morning the *Gray Ghost* weighed anchor and sailed out of the harbor and away from Tortuga. Both Horacio and Nick knew the fight was not over. It only had just begun.

sixteen
the ouija witch

In the middle of the island of Tortuga

CELESTIA CAME from a long line of Irish healers, and believed in the supernatural powers of prayer. Her grandmother was a devout Catholic, and Fox remembered how the sick would come to their home to visit with her nanna, Aurania. Her name meant Golden Lady in Gaelic. She was named after the daughter of an Irish chieftain, Donal Og McCarthy.

The *Black Widow* crew was prepared to set sail in two days. So, Celestia had scoured the rocky island for a fortuneteller who might provide them with a sneak peek at their future.

When Celestia was a child, her grandmother would lead sick visitors to her sitting parlor to pray. First, she would have them wait as she wrapped a raw egg with white thread from a special spool. She tirelessly mumbled verses from the Bible as she wrapped the shell over and over until nothing was visible but white string.

Then, her nanna would lay it on the coals of the wood-burning stove and the praying would continue.

As she prayed, the flames caressed the magical egg until the white thread turned black. Then, she would remove the egg from the glowing cinders. If it stayed whole, the visitor would be healed. If it collapsed, the guest would not survive their sickness.

When her granddaughter questioned her nanna about the ritual, the old woman said she could save only those worthy with prayer.

Sometimes, people would come to her grandmother to discover what lay in their future even though they were free of ailments. The ritual would be repeated. So, Celestia thought nothing of seeking providence from an island healer. Perhaps she would be forewarned of any dangers that awaited them on their upcoming voyage.

Only Nick, Celestia, Skinny, and Willy went to find the woman some called a witch. Horacio's disability prevented him from accompanying his friends on their quest; he could not climb the rocky cliffs where the religious woman was said to live. With the Hammer's blessing, Nick led the foursome into the hills to hear what was in store for them on their maiden voyage.

The trek took nearly the entire morning as they climbed hill after hill. Frequently, they had to cut their way through the dense vegetation with machetes, slowing their progress considerably. Celestia insisted they continue, and they struggled until they spotted a plume of smoke in the distance. Nick was first to see the hut and signaled the group to stop.

"It looks like it's just over that rise," Nick whispered.

"Why are you whispering?" Celestia asked and chuckled lightly. "Are you afraid of ghosts and witches?"

"No, of course not," Nick said as his neck turned red and his voice sounded like he wasn't so sure of himself.

Celestia laughed and skipped ahead without a care. The hut appeared to be made of palm fronds and bamboo. There was a hole in the center of the roof where a stream of black smoke rose. As they approached, a pungent odor filled the air, and they could hear a voice chanting inside the tiny shack.

The shabby dwelling gave Celestia pause; it wasn't what she had expected. Somehow, she thought she would find a more conventional structure, one similar to Nanna's on the Irish countryside. This looked more like a witch's den than the respite of a religious healer. The young girl glanced at Nick, then at Willy and Skinny. It was obvious she was questioning her decision.

Celestia had no intention of turning back without learning about their future, though. So, she took a deep breath, nodded and led the way forward.

When they reached the doorway, they all stopped. Their hearts beat like hammers and their eyes were spread as wide as saucers when Celestia pushed aside a tattered curtain that served as a door. As she peered into the dark room, the smell became overpowering. It left a bitter taste in her mouth. An old woman, head bent over a pot, stood before a glowing fire. As she stirred, steam clouded her head and an orange glow reflected on her face.

"Excuse me, ma'am," Celestia said in just over a whisper.

When the woman looked up, all Celestia could see was the whites of her eyes. Obviously, the woman was blind, but she appeared to have sensed their presence. As they approached, she lifted her head and seemed to smell her visitors. Lids blinked over sightless eyes several times, and she cackled in a way that sent cold chills up the spines of all four of them.

"Come here and sit down," the old woman said in a voice cracked with age.

When Celestia edged forward, the ancient woman said, "You three, as well."

The comment startled the men because they had not spoken a word. Yet the woman clearly was aware of their presence. Immediately, Nick guessed they were getting involved in some sort of black magic. If not for the brave insistence of Celestia, he would have turned and left as fast as possible. His Irish friend was adamant they gain insight about their future before embarking on such an important adventure.

Celestia looked back at Nick, Skinny, and Willy and motioned for them to comply. With hesitation, all sat around a wooden table. The top was ornately decorated with ivory inlay. The table alone was worth more than a hundred of the huts in which the strange woman lived. On the top, left corner of the table was the word *YES*. On the top right was the word *No*. The alphabet was displayed in two arcs in the middle, while another row contained the numbers one through ten. The woman explained it was a Ouija board.

Of course, Celestia was aware such boards had been used by the Egyptians and earlier people. Although she had never seen one, she had heard the tales of the strange messages they were capable of providing. In her family, it was a forbidden possession and considered a tool of Satan.

She also had heard spirit boards were praised for their accuracy in foretelling the future. So, they sat patiently, waiting for the witch to say more.

In the middle of the inlaid table was a planchette that looked like a heart-shaped piece of wood.

"Each of you put two fingers on the planchette," the blind woman said.

Nick looked from Skinny to Willy and back to Celestia. His face was filled with doubt and a twinge of fear. The fortuneteller had done nothing to calm his nerves or alleviate his uncertainty.

"Now, tell me what it is you want to know," the witch asked.

Celestia looked deep into Nick's eyes, then she replied, "Will we return to Tortuga after our journey?"

As soon as the words escaped her mouth, the wooden planchette started to move all on its own. Each of the friends looked suspiciously at the other, believing one of them was making it move. But no one had done more than lay the tips of their fingers on the wooden planchette. It slid across the table on its own, moved by some unseen power. The witch was not touching it, although her sightless eyes seemed to follow its path.

As the planchette moved across the table, it finally stopped over the word, *YES*. Celestia's eyes sparkled. She looked at Nick and said, "I told you so."

"Go ahead and ask it something else," Nick said, urging her on. "Ask if we will return with vast riches and at what cost."

As soon as Nick said the words, the wooden planchette began to move again. First it stopped on the word, *yes*. Then it glided across the board and hovered over a letter and paused briefly only to move again until it located another letter. This was repeated a number of times as it traveled across the table and finally stopped at a number. Visible through the hole in the top of the planchette was the number *2*. Celestia reached into her britches and pulled out a two-bit pencil and a yellow piece of paper. She scribbled down letter after letter from each stop. When the planchette halted its journey, Celestia turned the paper for her friends to read. She had written, *"LIVES WILL BE LOST - 2."*

Celestia looked at the table as her mouth dropped open. Then she asked, "Who will die?"

But the wooden planchette didn't move. Nobody removed their fingers from the heart-shaped piece of wood as they all stared hard at the middle of the table, where it came to rest. What they had learned was too shocking not to try to find out more. But the Ouija would not cooperate. They sat quietly and waited. Seconds turned into minutes, and minutes turned into an hour.

Finally, the blind witch said, "It has nothing more to say. You will have to wait to find out what the future holds."

Then, the old woman stretched out her hand with her palm up. She demanded one piece of silver for her services. Celestia reached into her pocket and pulled out a coin that sparkled despite the dim light. When she placed it in her wrinkled hand, the old woman breathed a backward sigh and clucked like a hen. She put the coin between her teeth and bit hard, confirming its value. Then, she returned to the earthenware pot and again began stirring. The pungent smell intensified as she mixed the vile concoction with a long wooden spoon.

Finally, Celestina nudged Nick and whispered, "Let's get out of here. This woman makes me feel like ghosts are at our backs. Maybe coming here wasn't such a good idea after all."

seventeen
cat & mouse

In the Caribbean Sea

WHEN THE *BLACK Widow* hoisted sails and began to slip out of the harbor, the crew's excitement was apparent. Thirty-nine men and one woman were aboard to tend to the needs of the ship. The original ten were not only thrilled about the coming adventure; they were in awe at all they had achieved. It wasn't so long ago, they were orphans and castoffs with no apparent chance in life. By sheer will, they turned things around for the better. Now they were a tightly knit group of loyal friends on the brink of a brand-new start.

Horacio and Nick smiled from the ship's helm. Hammer spun the massive pilot's wheel, tacking the *Black Widow* in a southwesterly direction toward the coast of South America. A steady stream of cargo ships sailed to and from the Spanish-held continent, carrying everything from livestock and grain to pottery. On rare occasions, some of the holds secretly were filled with chests of gold and silver.

The crew of the *Black Widow* was more focused on their first grand adventure than valuable coins. Most paramount for them was reputation. The value of plundered cargo was secondary.

Each of the newly enlisted men kept a keen eye on Horacio and Nick because their future depended on their actions. They knew both men possessed lightning-quick tempers. The Texan, especially, was easily enticed to anger and action. Hammer was slightly more tempered, and he knew how to rein in his cowboy friend.

The captain and first mate were alert and fastidious as they approached the dangerous waters Spanish warships were known to traverse. Horacio embarked on the voyage meticulously. He gleaned information from a variety of sources, including captains of smaller fishing vessels which frequently stopped at nearby islands and gathered information on the comings and goings of the Spanish fleet and other cargo ships.

The large cargo haulers would be their primary targets, and the *Black Widow* had an armory large enough to succeed. The ship's cannon would not match Queen Isabela's warships gun for gun, but Horacio knew cunning would play a major part of a successful raid. And he believed that was where the valuables would be hidden. Only warships would be given the responsibility of carrying the most precious items back to the European Continent.

The last sighting of a Spanish man-of-war was made

a hundred miles south of the Colombian island of San Andres. It supposedly had disembarked from Cartagena. So, it was in that direction they sailed. With less draft than the Spanish vessels, the *Black Widow* was more agile than the heavy warships.

Horacio instructed Nick to tend the helm and hug the coast in waters too shallow for the Spanish Armada to navigate. With the South American coast as a backdrop, the *Black Widow* became less conspicuous and her discovery near impossible.

When the trade winds faltered, and the ship's speed was reduced to a snail's pace, Horacio directed it to a coastal anchorage. As they stopped for the night, the captain ordered all lights doused and guards to take stations around the ship and high in the masts. As they spent the night in front of an impenetrable coast of dense jungle, they spotted no sign of running lights seaward.

When morning neared, a light haze showed on the eastern horizon. Soon streaks of orange, red, and yellow shot across the sky like fangs from a giant beast. Light unfolded across the sea like a blanket, unveiling what might have been hidden by darkness. As flickering stars gave way to sunlight, the crow's nest sounded the alarm.

The top sails of a ship were spotted on the distant horizon. Horacio ordered the crew to make no unnecessary noise. Sound traveled easily across calm water. The lookout dropped a length of rope to the deck to get the first mate's attention.

Nick was resting beside Captain Hellsworth, when

the thump of hemp hitting the deck made them look up. When they looked to the crow's nest, the man pointed to the horizon. From the deck, the earth's curve blocked their view. So, both Nick and Horacio quickly scaled the webbing that led to the high masts.

Horacio climbed the rope ladder faster than Nick because his powerful arms and back were used to the strain of the rigging. His pegleg dangled as he pulled himself upward hand over hand.

The muscles in Nick's arms responded in kind. Both men had become hard and powerful in the last months. Their physiques no longer were those of gangly boys. They were men on an important mission.

When at sea, every yard of height increased a sailor's vision by another mile. When Nick and Horacio were some sixty feet above the *Black Widow's* deck, they could just make out a wavering image at the water's edge.

They both employed collapsible spy glasses and looked to the horizon, hoping to identify the passing vessel. They immediately saw the Spanish flag high on one of its three masts. It was a man-of-war.

Nick looked from the sea to Horacio and back at the sea. He grinned and asked, "Should we run from it or attack, amigo?"

"Neither!" Horacio said thoughtfully. "If we trail the ship at the same distance we are now; we may be able to shadow her and discover where she is headed. If she changes course and heads our way, we can easily outmaneuver such a large ship. We'll cling to the shallow waters where she won't dare venture. It will be harder to see us with land behind us; our chances of discovery will be less than if we are at sea."

Nick nodded as he understood Horacio's reasoning. Neither of them had the experience of some crewmen, but Hammer's mind was like a mousetrap. Once he learned or even read something, it stayed in his memory forever. A Dutch doctor on the island had told him it was called a photographic memory.

Hellsworth studied the Spanish sailing ship at length, while Nick scanned the horizon for other vessels. He smiled when he spotted a second ship several miles behind the man-of-war. High above the vessel flew a familiar black flag with the skull and crossbones. The Spanish were entirely unaware Captain Zachery Banshee was on their tail. Nick grinned a little more.

"This must be our lucky day," he said with a chuckle. "That son-of-a-bitch, Banshee, is dogging the warship. I wonder what he's up to?"

"Probably the same thing we are," Horacio replied.

"I wouldn't take it kindly if Zachery Banshee plundered that ship before we did."

"Don't worry, mate," Horacio said. "He has a lot of cannons, but when it comes to maneuvering, he's rubbish compared to us. He'll never match us running in shallow water and close to the wind."

The *Black Widow* hugged the Colombian coast as they trailed the ships in a game of cat and mouse. The rookies decided to leave their prey alone until one or the others made a move.

"That is the moment to strike," Horacio explained.

"When their attention is focused elsewhere, they'll never see us coming."

The *Black Widow* glided through the water as the trade winds tugged at her sails, pushing her farther away from home and toward an uncertain destiny. The Colombian coast was also known for its pirates and marauders. Every thief in South America was aware of what the Spaniards had been doing for the last two hundred years.

Queen Isabella II was pressing her officers to collect every last bit of gold and silver the natives of the primitive lands could provide. Greed was making passage through the vast ocean waters more dangerous. Pirates and thieves roamed the land and sea, determined to steal the last of the spoils and escape to safe waters.

On the third day, the slow-moving Spanish war ship pulled into the island of San Andres. Even though the Colombian island was ruled by the Spanish, it was closer to Central America than it was to South America. The island was discovered on the second voyage of Christopher Columbus.

The first conquistadors to set foot on San Andres were Alonso de Ojeda and Pedro de Nicuesa. The surrounding islands were in what was called the "The Sea of Seven Colors," and provided safe harbor for pirates over the last century. None dared to breach the main island due to the Spanish Armada's presence. The Spanish were powerful, even though many believed their superiority was coming to an end. Other navies, those of the British Empire and the United States of America, were about to claim world domination.

eighteen
sea of seven colors

Off the Coast of Central America

THE CREW of the *Black Widow* lay on a beach, letting the early sun sink into their skin and chase away the chill of a night on the open sea. While they waited for breakfast to be prepared, Horacio and Nick climbed to the top of Providencia, an isle just five miles long, and stood watch for the Spanish warship. They knew the *Gray Ghost* had gone into hiding as it waited for the ship to reemerge and set sail for Fuerteventura in the Canary Islands. The seven Spanish islands, located off the coast of eastern Africa, would be the last stop before the Spanish man-of-war returned home and to the naval port of Cadiz.

The sandy beach was steep and emptied into an exquisite sea of turquoise. Brown patches showed parts of the reef in the depths and a multitude of fish flashed bright colors in the shallows. The Caribbean Sea and the sky melted into one on the curved horizon. The water was as calm as a millpond without the stir of a single breeze. Seagulls hovered just over the surface dipping their beaks into the bubbling water where a ball of fish futilely attempted to escape the hungry jaws of a school of yellowfin tuna. They gobbled up dozens of the sardines with each pass.

"With no wind, they won't be leaving the island anytime soon," Skinny Razor said as he gazed out to sea and frowned.

"You best watch what you wish for and not be in such a rush to see battle," Aldo Rey said. "I am from Spain. Be assured, if we run into any conquistadores, they may well be more than we can handle. They conquered the entire South American Continent with less than two hundred men on horses."

"I'd like to catch me one of those fancy officers myself," Wishbone said. "They was the ones who took Hambone and me from our parents."

"Where's your family now, Wish?" Willy asked.

"We never saw them again," Wishbone replied as he frowned. "They were sold and shipped off on a different boat. We were lucky we were kept together. It's 'cause we're so small most folks wouldn't buy us."

"You both may well be on the short side, but you don't have a dandling nature, that's for sure," Jack Fury said. "The pair of you work harder than any two of us. Those fools didn't know what they were looking at."

"That was just lucky for us," Hambone said with a grin. "If it weren't for Nick here, we'd be shipped to who knows where—maybe even split up or thrown overboard. I don't think I could make it without my brother."

"You both have seven brothers now," Skinny Razor said.

"And one sister," Celestia added.

The brothers' bright white teeth showed as they smiled, and the whites of their eyes stood out against their dark skin. Both were amazed by how the world had righted itself. Skinny Razor was right. They now had a passel of brothers and a sister that were orphans just like them.

It was often said, Nick Risk and Horacio Hellsworth led their gang of orphans astray. That was not the case at all. Those who knew them understood the horrors of their past lives. They all had been prisoners of one sort or another, even slaves. Neither Nick nor Horacio had ever ordered their friends to do anything they themselves wouldn't do. They certainly wouldn't oblige them to set sail on an adventure that would include piracy on the high seas if they chose not to go. All decided to follow of their own free will.

They all had heard how the conquistadores had demonized the South Americans with their cruel behavior. So, the crew of the *Black Widow* would not hesitate to strike the Spanish man-of-war. Their hearts were set on restitution for the wrongs inflicted on a helpless people by wicked men and tyrannical leaders.

Money was the one thing the orphan crew knew the least about. None of them had ever had any. Much like Horacio on the streets of London, what money they did secure was through thievery and deception.

If the *Black Widow* were able to seize a precious cargo, it would be the first time any of them had possessed any real wealth. Having a silver coin or two in one's pocket was extraordinary. Anything more would come as a blessing or miracle. To each man and one woman, the adventure they were about to embark upon was more valuable than the promise of riches.

Seated on a rocky mount, high above the small island's shoreline, Nick spotted movement in the morning hours. A good breeze had blown up that night and whitecaps glistened for as far as the eye could see. Finally, he saw the Spanish warship's masts depart the island refuge and set sail due east for the Atlantic Ocean.

The sun had just begun to peek over the eastern horizon. Nick pulled a small mirror from his jacket pocket and used the first rays of light to send a reflection off the mirror to Horacio, who sat on the beach with the other crewmembers.

It didn't take Horacio long to spot the flashing light from the summit. It brought the news they all had been waiting for, the departure of the warship from San Andres's Island. Nick raced down the hill to where his friends hastily were preparing to take the tender back to the ship and continue their pursuit of the Spanish vessel. They were convinced this ship was carrying something more than standard cargo because of its attempt to sneak out of the port in the early hours.

A Spanish man-of-war was more challenging to locate than an entire fleet of ships, so there was some logic in the vessel setting out alone, plus the Spanish had fewer resources than they had had just fifty years before. The Queen's Navy had been devastated by massive hurricanes off the coast of Florida and lost ships had yet to be replaced. The world's naval superpower was now in a downward spiral.

As soon as Nick's cowboy boots hit the sand, Horacio and the crew were ready to row back to the *Black Widow*. They decided to continue to pursue the warship at a distance, waiting to see what Captain Banshee had in mind. More than one cat was chasing the mouse.

nineteen
man-of-war

The Caribbean Sea

SPAIN WAS EXPERIENCING its last days of dominance in South America. It struggled to maintain its hold in order to steal vast amounts of gold and silver from the indigenous population of the continent. Their conquistadores swept across the lands as assassins, wiping out the tribal leaders, kings, and queens and recovering massive riches in the name of Isabela II, Queen of Spain. All of South America hated the Spaniards but, due to their advanced weaponry and naval might, could do little to repel the invaders.

The same vessels that protected the Spanish soldiers were used to cart priceless treasures back to Cadiz, making them the target of every pirate ship that sailed the Caribbean and the Atlantic Ocean. Frequently, the warships sailed in large flotillas, making it difficult to tell which ship was laden with treasure. Other times, they secretly made their way out of South American ports in an attempted to slip past the covetous bucca-neers. A lone ship on the vast Atlantic Ocean was hard to locate. Two-thirds of the earth's surface is made up of water, making it all but impossible to find or run into such a vessel.

With both the *Black Widow* and the *Gray Ghost* in secret pursuit, it was impossible for the man-of-war to disappear into the vastness of the ocean.

The trick to locating such a ship was to get inside information. Or even gossip that came from crew members in the taverns and pubs scattered across the harbors in the northern part of South America.

In the past, great fleets of Spanish warships sailed together to chaperone vessels laden with booty. Still, they had fallen to the extreme weather in the Americas, and many sank by one of the massive hurricanes that were prominent in this part of the world. And others were destroyed by enemy ships of the French or British.

This blow damaged their naval fleet and cost them vast fortunes when scores of gold bullion was lost at the bottom of the sea off the coast of Florida. Due to the reduced number of pirates on the high seas compared to the 16th and 17th centuries, they often took more chances and sent their fortunes in lone vessels as they had on that summer's day.

Attacking such a ship was no easy task. Some carried as many as eighty cannon and two hundred men. Choosing such an adversary required foolproof planning, something that wasn't lost on Hellsworth or Risk. They planned to deceive the floating fortress without arousing suspicion.

"Remember those sails we had made up just in case we had to run?" Risk asked his partner. "I believe now would be a good time to put 'em to use."

Horacio looked pensively at his first mate and paused before answering. When he nodded his approval, the crew sprang into action. Nick needed to only nod toward Willy and Skinny. They and other crewman were off to fetch the heavy sacks of cloth. A swarm of sailors immediately scrambled up the rigging and began pulling down one set of sails and raising another. It was amazing how quickly they did such a large and heavy task. But the crew now worked together like a fine Swiss watch. When the changeover was complete, the sight left the *Black Widow's* crew in awe.

As the breeze began to blow in earnest, they turned the fleet pirate ship toward the expected point of contact between the *Gray Ghost* and the Spanish warship. Hammer had the vessel cutting through the waters at almost eight knots. Eager eyes were cast toward the bow of the ship and the first sign of sails on the horizon. It took a few hours for the *Black Widow* to get near enough to see what was happening from the ship's deck.

Horacio was surprised to see their approach go unnoticed. Instead, the *Gray Ghost* and the Spanish man-of-war circled each other in preparation for imminent combat. Nick and Horacio felt somewhat helpless because they were so far away from the coming battle. They may not be friends with Captain Banshee, but he was still part of the pirate community of Tortuga. If needed, they would come to his aid. That appeared imminent, too

The distance between the *Black Widow* and the two ships facing off was about three miles. It would still be a good twenty minutes or more before they could assist the *Gray Ghost*.

Horacio commanded the crew to add cloth. He tacked closer to the wind and they gained two knots in speed. It was then the battery of cannons of the man-of-war opened up with a massive broadside attack. Flames and black smoke poured from the Spanish ship as it unloaded forty rounds of hot nuts and bolts at their enemy.

From a distance, they could see the shrapnel from the cannon blasts tear at the fabric of the *Gray Ghost's* sails. Another round of cannonball sheered the stern mast in two, crippling the pirate ship and littering the deck with debris and dead crewmen. With little regard for the damages, Banshee's ship returned fire. Blast after blast came from both ships as they moved closer until they were alongside each other.

Their blood running hot with excitement, five crewmen of the *Black Widow* ran to the gunwale to watch. An Englishman, Nigel Bumoney, cried out, "We've got to get to her to assist, Captain!"

"Duck your heads, mates," the Australian Royston Farrell shouted just before the cannonball hit the side of the *Black Widow*. "They're firing at us from the stern!"

The hot lead ball hit the top of the gunwale, careened and took off the heads of the Englishman and the Australian much like a guillotine. The other three crew members quickly dove for cover and lay flat on the deck when the shot hit. The impact made the *Black Widow* reverberate hard, but it did less damage than expected. The small size of the aft cannons and the distance they had to travel lessened the damage they could inflict.

It was the only shot fired at Captain Hellsworth's vessel. When the two warring ships saw the *Black Widow* bearing down on them, the combat stopped as crewmen stared out in shock and horror. Both batteries of cannon went silent as the sailors on both ships stared wide-eyed into the smoky mist. Some of the Europeans jumped overboard and tried to swim away from the doom that approached.

As if it was sailing out of the setting sun and a fiery red sky, the *Black Widow* advanced in the afternoon haze. Its red sails appeared to be dripping the blood of the dead sailors.

A lone figure, wearing a Texan hat and brandishing two pistols, stood at the bow. His eyes were as fiery red as the ship's canvas, and he grinned like a hungry jackal. Without hesitation, First Mate Risk swung the mid-sized cannon, mounted on the bow, toward the pilot at the Spanish war ship's helm. Then he put the tip of his cheroot to the wick and the small gun fired.

Flames spewed from the barrel as a shot was sent up the Spanish ship's spout. It was a direct hit. The salvo instantly killed the pilot and damaged the wheel. The Spanish vessel was rendered helpless and adrift as the *Black Widow* pulled up along its broadside. Immediately, the Spanish captain ordered his crew to strike a white flag of surrender.

The crew of the *Gray Ghost* was surprised to see it was the pirates from Tortuga who had caught the Spanish in a crossfire. They had deceived the enemy with their red sails and ended the battle with a single cannon blast. Cheers went up from the crews of both pirate ships. Grappling hooks were tossed from each side of the man-of-war, and pirates immediately swarmed the decks of the *Perla de Sevilla*. Captain Banshee's boots hit the Spanish deck at just about the same time Horacio's pegleg hammered on the wood. Nick was right behind him.

"Well, Zachery," Horacio said with a huge smile. "As the Americans say, I believe we saved your bacon."

The *Gray Ghost* captain could not deny the fact, but that didn't mean he liked it. Especially when rules of the sea dictated the spoils would be split. To the buccaneers' surprise, it turned out the *Perla de Sevilla was* one of the select Spanish vessels that was laden with thousands of pounds of silver and gold. The riches exceeded all of their dreams, even those of Captain Banshee.

The crew hoisted one chest after another of silver jewelry, coins and bricks of gold to the main deck. The riches were so vast no one dared comprehend what it all was worth. Surely, it was more than they had ever imagined.

Horacio eyed the Spanish captain and asked, "And now what should we do with the ship and crew?"

"How about we take the captain with us to stand

trial for atrocities committed against innocent people," Razor suggested. "Quite a few South Americans are living in Tortuga. Most will seek restitution. Then, we can let the rest of crew go home or wherever they choose to flee."

"And give away the ship we just captured?" Willy questioned with shock-filled eyes.

"There's no need to be greedy," Nick said. "If we take the ship, what would we do with the crew? It's one thing to seize a Spanish ship, and it is quite another to needlessly kill all the men aboard. What they do from here on out is up to them. I say let everybody go but the captain. He'll be the one responsible for any wrongdoing. He and the pilot, but he's already dead from the cannon blast. The ships busted up anyway. It'll take a day to get something rigged up just to steer it. I say we cut 'em loose."

"We need to split up the booty and run for safety," Banshee said with a hint of disrespect. "But you won't be getting half of anything. My offer is seventy-thirty. That's it. Take it or leave it."

"Seventy-thirty is a generous offer," Nick said as he began to laugh. "I never thought you'd be so big-hearted. Thank ya, partner."

"Not seventy percent for you, fool!" Banshee spat. "You should consider yourself fortunate to get anything at all, pup."

Nick's hands were a blur as he pulled his Collier wheel-pistols and put two bullets into Zachery's hat, kicking it into the air. In mid-flight, he put another pair of rounds into it, propelling the cap even farther into the sky. The pirate captain was so startled at the American's quick action that he stood there with his mouth open. The arrogant captain quickly realized he was standing at the devil's door.

"The way I see it," Nick said with a grin that would make a possum jealous, "you're lucky not to be at the bottom of the sea in Davy Jones's locker. If it weren't for our tricking the Spanish into thinking we be ghosts from the Flying Dutchman, we'd have never gotten the drop on 'em. But we did, and you didn't. You were just about to be sunk. Our marksmanship wasn't at all shabby, either. We knocked out the pilot's wheel with one shot."

As Horacio neared the two, his pegleg resounded on the deck of the Spanish ship. He had a fire in his eye, and it was shooting daggers at Banshee.

"Who the hell do you think you are?" Hammer roared. "I have a mind to throw you overboard and feed you to the sharks."

Zachary went to protest again, but he suddenly felt the hot blade of a knife at his neck, and a woman's voice whispered into his ear.

"How would you like to die right here?" Celestia asked in a whisper. "Don't worry. We still will give your crew their fair share. Fifty-fifty is what it's going to be. Just like it says in the pirate charter, written over a century ago. You can follow the rules or argue from the bottom of the ocean."

Banshee was so taken aback he shook his head as his heart pounded. "Fifty-fifty it is then," he said hoarsely. "Now, can you put the knife down?"

Even though the pirate captain was seething, he held his tongue. He recognized the *Black Widow* crew would not be intimidated, and they were capable of killing him. They had the advantage and earned an even split of the spoils. Each crew took their share, boarded their respective ships and set sail in opposite directions.

Banshee left with his pride wounded but still a wealthy man. It was clear to all, though, his scrap with the young pirates was far from over. The orphan crew had indeed won the day, but that didn't necessarily mean they would triumph over Captain Zachery Banshee in the future. He was an enemy for whom they must be wary.

The defeated Latin crew turned their ship for the closest Spanish settlement outside the Americas—the Canary Islands. Luckily. there was a man on board who had studied as a pilot. He worked out a course with dead reckoning to find a safe harbor. His task was not difficult. The African coast was due east. When the coast of Africa was in sight, they would turn north until they ran into Fuerteventura, the nearest island to the continent. From there, they would go no farther.

There were no conquistadores aboard, so all of the sailors were allowed their freedom, a considerable reward for a member of the Spanish Armada. All saw the writing in the sand. They realized Spain's time of dominating the world was over and only defeat lay in the future. After months at sea, all the Spanish wanted was to return to their homes and their own kind. They cared little for the lost treasure; it wasn't theirs anyway.

They were thankful they had surrendered to honorable pirates.

There was no sorrow over the loss of a tyrannical captain. They knew he would be ransomed and sent back to the queen. They happily were free of oppression.

The orphans huddled together once they had set sail for Tortuga. Donk sat on the deck with his legs crossed. His white rat ran up his arm and sat on his shoulder. Willy had found some sweets in the Spanish galley and was nibbling on a candy cane.

On the floor before them lay several samples of the riches they had acquired—a few silver and gold bars, a dozen precious stones and some jewelry. They were all left speechless as they stared at the riches. None of them had words to justify their new-found wealth.

twenty
flying dutchman

Just Over the Horizon

NOT FAR FROM the site of the battle sailed a lone ship that cast no shadow. It cut through the sea but made no sound. At the helm was Captain Hendrick Van der Decken. He had nearly a hundred men in his charge. As they moved about the deck and climbed the rigging to tend to the sails, their images were hazy and ghost-like. It was almost as if they weren't there at all.

The sails flapped in the windless night as the current pushed at the hull. It was the only audible sound and the only indication the ship wasn't a mirage or the figment of a weary sailor's imagination. It appeared to float just above the water instead of in it.

Many sailors thought the ghost ship was some sort of doomsday vessel. In fact, it had been seen in all of the Seven Seas as it beaconed unsuspecting seamen to their doom. Any sailors who set eyes on it were said to soon meet their death. The captain and crew of the ghost ship lived in a sort of purgatory. They existed neither among the living world nor in heaven or hell. They roamed somewhere in between, cursed to sail the world's seas and oceans for eternity.

Captain Van der Decken stood at the ghost ship's helm with the sails the color of blood. Of course, the Dutch master had sailed the seas of the earth for so long no one alive remembered when it had all begun. Still graceful, the doomsday ship cut through the waters as the wind filled its sails.

The tale of the *Flying Dutchman* goes back centuries. The first time the ship was seen, it was at the Cape of Storms during the lifetime of a European sailor named Pascua de Gambas. The last sighting was by the Portuguese in 1821. It was said the ship glowed with a ghostly light. When crews boarded her, death struck like a whaler's harpoon. None survived.

Years ago, at the Cape of Storms, off the southern coast of South Africa, the *Dutchman* encountered a storm so violent the crew begged Captain Van der Decken to turn for shore.

The captain was said to reply, "May I be eternally damned if I do, though I should beat about her till the day of judgment."

Due to his stubbornness, all of the ship's hands were lost at sea. The captain's declarations to heaven and hell were consummated, and he and the crew were destined to sail the earth till the end of time.

The phantom ship had been seen time after time but never east of the Cape of Storms. Doom followed each sighting. Some vessels simply disappeared; others later were found crewless and adrift. Bad luck befell them all.

When the *Black Widow* brought down the Spanish man-of-war, the *Flying Dutchman* was just over the horizon. Whether Captain Hendrick Van der Decken was aware two pirate ships had engaged the Spaniards will never be known. But disaster lay in wait for one.

A Spanish sailor reportedly saw the phantom ship disappear over the horizon as it trailed the *Gray Ghost*. The future of Captain Banshee and his crew was undetermined, as was the fate of all those who lived by the pirate code on the high seas.

The *Black Widow's* crew of orphans was far luckier than they imagined. For those who see the red sails of the Flying Dutchman were doomed along with their ship.

twenty-one
friends &
enemies

The Island of Tortuga

WHEN THE BLACK Widow and her crew weighed anchor in the harbor of Cayona, the sun was just setting over the island of Tortuga. A haze lay heavy with moisture in the summer air, magnifying the moon to unseen proportions. As it suddenly rose into the sky, shadows were cast on the west side of the deck, and it seemed so close one could reach out and caress its craters.

The constellations stood bright in the evening sky. Suddenly a series of comets raced across the heavens, leaving heat trails that went from west to east and finally disappeared behind the horizon. The chain rattled as the lever released the lock, dropping the anchor into the harbor's depths.

When the crown of the anchor hit the sand and the bill took hold, the ship swung around, leaving the bow pointing into the wind. There was a flurry of movement as sails were stowed, and the crew made ready to drop the rowboats in the gently breathing sea.

"What did you do with the Spanish captain?" Horacio asked Celestia.

"He's locked in the brig, but he doesn't have a scratch on him. He's even been fed food and wine. Should I bring him on deck?"

"I reckon we best keep him and our plunder aboard the *Black Widow* until we figure out what to do with 'em," Nick said.

"As the captain doesn't speak a word of English, I'll tend to him," Aldo Rey said with a smirk. "We can discuss at length the future of the once-great Spanish Empire. Maybe I can find out how important he is. Then, we will know how much ransom he's worth."

"Until now, he hasn't even given us his name," Celestia said. "The man is as mute as a tree stump."

"Make sure you see he doesn't come to any harm or doesn't hurt himself for that matter," Horacio said. "The Spanish royalty will pay less for damaged goods and be a heap more eager to seek revenge. I believe if we treat him well, it will simply be a business transaction."

"Don't worry, Captain," Aldo said. "This is about money and nothing more. I've got my priorities straight."

The bullion they had found in the hold of the *Peal of Sevilla* was immense, far more than the thousand pounds they had initially believed. There were so many chests of gold, silver, and jeweled trinkets, it would take several days to remove it all from the ship and move it into town.

As a result, the *Black Widow's* sat lower in the water during her homeward journey. It left her vulnerable to storms and attack. The weight of the plunder doubled her draft and mandated the *Widow* navigate in deeper water, where they were more likely to be spotted. Ever cautious, Hammer preferred a lighter load and hugging the coastline. He doubled the watch.

As Horacio had promised, they returned without incident and looked forward to a bright future. They assumed Captain Banshee had set a course for Port Royal and Jamaica, another safe haven for pirates in the Caribbean Sea.

Of the forty-man crew, only two remained aboard the ship. Aldo and Donk stayed behind to ensure no one else came aboard and nobody neared the brig. They were also there to make sure no one entered the hold that held the gold and silver.

The captain, first mate, Celestia, and five of their friends tended the oars of the longboat as they made their way to the beach. They carried with them one wooden chest of valuables from the Spanish man-of-war.

Of course, the word of their arrival spread through Cayona like wildfire. It appeared the entire town arrived to welcome their friends home. Many of the spectators held torches, illuminating the beach. The flames flickered and made their shadows appear to dance across the sand. At the head of the welcoming committee, of course, stood the governor, Captain Blade.

"Welcome home, family," Blade said as he flashed

his white teeth with open arms. "You're all back sooner than expected. Did you run into any trouble?"

"We ran into Captain Banshee," Skinny said. "He was in the middle of a battle with the *Pearl of Sevilla*, a Spanish warship."

Blade let out a long whistle and said, "I've heard of her. She is said to have eighty guns."

"She was just about to sink the *Gray Ghost* and all," Nick added. "We were obliged to save her along with the crew and captain."

With raised eyebrows, Captain Blade replied, "Is that so? I would have paid a shiny piece of silver to see Banshee's face. Had it been me, I may have let Zachary sink with his ship."

"What? We would have missed the discomfort we inflicted by saving his skin," Horacio said and laughed. "No, sir, it was a grand moment."

"Boys, bring the treasure chest, will ya?" Nick said as his grin widened. "The look on Banshee's face when he had to accept what had happened was priceless."

"We split the booty, and I reckon he sailed for Jamaica," Horacio said. "I'm sure when he arrives at Port Royal, he'll say he defeated the Spanish man-of-war all on his own."

"It wouldn't surprise me at all," Captain Blade said and joined in with the laughter. "But the truth of such matters seldom takes long to come to light. What did you do with the *Pearl of Sevilla*?"

"We gave her to the crew," Nick said. "We figured it wise not to steal one of Queen Isabella's ships or she might send her conquistadores after us."

"And the captain?" Captain Blade asked. "I believe his name is Javier Perez de Castellon. A famous man in Europe."

"We've got him on board the *Black Widow*," Nick said. "But we ain't touched a hair on his head. We only want the ransom."

"That should be easily arranged just across the water in Haiti," Blade said as he grinned some more. "Although it may be costly in time due to the distance to Spain, I would be delighted if you would allow me to take charge of the transaction. There could be political advantages to be had here, which would be good for the island."

"You're the boss, gov," the tall Texan said. "You'll know better how to go about it anyway."

"It will be just like the old days," Boris said and rubbed his hands together. "And here I thought we were looking at the last days of our pirate way of life."

"Not by a long shot, Captain," Nick said. "I'd venture to say our lives have just begun."

Willy, Aldo, Wishbone, and Hambone all struggled to lift the treasure chest from the rowboat. They grabbed the handles at either end as their faces turned red and veins pulsated at their temples. Sweat beaded up on their foreheads as they wrestled the heavy box out of the boat and onto the beach. When Nick strode over and opened the lid, the gold, silver, and precious stones sparkled in the light of the moon and torches.

Nick pulled both of his pistols and shot eight rounds into the sky to celebrate. Flames shot from the barrels of his wheel-guns, momentarily adding illumination to the night.

As the evening grew later, campfires were made and whole pigs roasted over hot coals. Somebody brought along fireworks, discovered in the back of the warehouse. They had been stolen from a Chinese junk a decade earlier, but the powder was still dry. Dozens of rockets were set in the sand and lit. They soared into the sky and finally burst into multicolored palm trees.

The celebration marked a new beginning for the orphans and the rest of the crew of the *Black Widow*. They had come full circle. At last, one and all were real pirates.

twenty-two
meaning of freedom

The Texas Saloon on Tortuga

AS THE ORIGINAL ten friends sat around a large table set off to one side in the Texas Saloon, Hambone appeared to be deep in thought. The warped windows distorted the objects outside, making them waver in the night and almost seem unreal. Each of the young men and a lone woman were trying to absorb the reality of the riches they had just acquired. Their capture of the *Peral of Sevilla* made them the wealthiest people on the island, and that included Blade, the governor.

In the past, he was a man who was looked on suspiciously by both Nick and Horacio. In the end, he had turned out to be the most honorable man on the island. It proved; one can never judge a man by the first impression. Even the tall, blonde Texan had changed his mind about Boris. It requires a good amount of character for men to admit when they are wrong. Risk recognized his error, and the two became fast friends.

"Whatcha thinkin' about there, Wish?" Nick asked.

"I just realized what it means to be free," Wishbone said with a bewildered look on his face. "When we were still slaves, we had heard the word often enough, but we never really knew how it would feel or how it would change everything. Hell, we hardly knew what the word meant. Since it was a dream so far out of reach, it never crossed my mind to consider the possibilities or implications."

The quick thinking of both black men amazed the rest of the group. They had learned so much in their last months on the island and aboard the *Black Widow*. It turned out, hidden behind the fear to speak freely, were two brilliant minds. The brothers tried to subdue their wisdom as slaves. Smart black men were considered dangerous by most owners.

"I reckon all of us feel a bit of that, amigo," Nick said and smiled. "I was wanted by the law and would have been sent to jail for who knows how many years. Willy, too. We made a mistake that might have cost us or freedom and possibly our lives."

"There are many types of slavery," Celestia said as she tilted her head back and looked up at the stars through the open window.

The heavens pulsated as the cosmos slowly moved across the sky. A large moon shone through the open window and cast shadows on their backs. An owl hooted in the night and the aroma of freshly perked coffee came from the saloon's kitchen.

"What would have happened to me were I not rescued? My fate would have been worse than death,"

Celestia said as she closed her eyes and remembered her close call with prostitution. "I would have been held in a brothel until I was used up and no longer of value to powerful owners. Then, I would have been cast aside like useless rubbish. Many of the girls tricked into the trade end up living on the streets of London and die of starvation."

Skinny blinked his eyes as he thought back on what he had expected after being arrested.

"I was bound for the gallows," Skinny said. "I reckon being dead is a might worse than being owned."

"Why ponder on our dark pasts?" Horacio said as he patted Celestia's shoulder. She opened her eyes as a tear ran down her cheek. "We all are rich now. We've gone from being paupers to being wealthy beyond our wildest dreams. And we've had a hell of an adventure doing so. I figure everything that has happened to each of us was woven into the destiny that brought us here. I feel the future is written in stone and no one can change it. I've always believed we must make the best of what we have and where we are. What is to come, most likely will come anyway, no matter what we do. At the end of it all, our lives are no more than a single drop of water in the vast ocean."

Willy blinked his eyes as if he were confused and said, "You mean if all of those bad things hadn't happened to us, we wouldn't be where we are now? I always thought bad luck was like a disease. Those of us who got it could never get rid of it. I guess I was wrong."

"So, what do you think the governor will get for the

captain of the *Pearl of Sevilla*?" Aldo Rey asked. "I figure the queen will pay heavily to get him back. It will be a tricky transaction because they know we are here, but the island's defenses make approach by a warship impossible."

"The complication will be how to trade him for silver or gold and not get caught in the process," Nick said. "That is why it is best left in the hands of Captain Blade."

"As long as he comes to no harm, I believe they will pay the ransom and be done with it," Rey said. "The Spanish ruler's days are numbered. They already have lost control of half the countries in South America. Eventually, they will lose Cuba, Haiti and Puerto Rico, too. It is just a matter of time.

"Before the Spanish, the Romans ruled. Before Romans, the Greeks and Egyptians reigned. There always will be a dominant power in the world. Spain's rule has ended. So, I don't foresee them taking revenge on us as long as the captain is delivered healthy and in a good frame of mind. The Spanish, Portuguese, and the French have been exchanging prisoners for decades."

"Do we really know how much money we have?" Skinny asked, scratching his head. "I've never seen a silver dollar before now, not alone chests full of gold and silver coins."

"I never thought that a boy from Cornwall could become rich," Jack Fury added. He was amazed by what they had accomplished. "I always believed a man had to be born into wealth. I was wrong, wasn't I? Before we escaped, I expected Nightingale, the brutal first mate of the British Royal Navy, would be the death of us all. It was a stroke of luck we got a chance to jump ship."

Donk sat quietly, pleased as punch as he played with his white rat, Pepe. He was a brute of a man and not a great thinker. He was born to be a follower, but he was as loyal a follower any man would ever want.

"I don't look into things so much," he said with a smile. "I really don't care where or how I got rich. All I know is that I am a free man, and I don't have to struggle to survive anymore. I reckon I could buy anything I want."

"And what is that, Donk?" Nick asked.

Donk didn't answer. He looked more puzzled than ever.

"What is it you plan to buy or do with all that money you've earned?" Nick repeated.

Magee looked at the first mate like he still didn't quite understand the question and said, "I never really thought about it until you mentioned it. I just figured not having to struggle to survive is plenty for me. But something will come to mind with time."

twenty-three
the new governor

Cayona, Tortuga

THE BLACK WIDOW crew had been on the island for over a year and had integrated into the population. They put their wealth to good use, building a small hospital and an orphanage for the young children of Tortuga who had nowhere to call home. They didn't want other young people to suffer as they had.

Captain Blade helped Nick and Horacio build a meeting hall for the Brethren of the Coast, the organization that designed the original pirate charter centuries earlier. Nick liked to call it a home for resident outlaws. Any disputes that arose were dealt with there. It also would become the center for decision-making by island leaders. All decisions, approved or disapproved, were final, based on the laws established on the island two hundred years earlier.

Celestia was placed in charge of the treasury, and

Willy oversaw the new warehouse. Hambone and Wishbone worked alongside them.

The Texas Saloon became the town's favorite tavern, and it kept Nick and Horacio busy. It is where they spent most of their time when not at sea.

Several months had passed since the *Black Widow* faced off with the Spanish warship. Three pirate ships were visiting Tortuga and were anchored in Cayona Bay.

The gang of orphans had brought fame to the small town, and it was busy for a weeknight. Everyone, including visiting buccaneers, obeyed the pirate code of years past. If they did not honor the island's laws, they knew they would lose a major source to sell their plundered valuables. None were willing to bite the hand that fed them.

Of course, Tortuga was one of the last places in the world where men and women of the trade could live in peace, knowing some world power wouldn't storm their island and hang them all. But any pirates caught at sea would face more grave consequences.

The captain of the *Pearl of Sevilla* eventually was set free without a ransom. With the help of Captain Blade, he was returned to Spain via the nearby island of Haiti. In return, Blade negotiated an agreement with the Spanish that gave the inhabitants of Tortuga and its waters immunity and freedom to come and go as they pleased. The only condition was that Tortuga's pirates would refrain from attacking Spanish ships in Caribbean waters. When Captain Blade walked into the Texas Saloon, he was immediately greeted by Nick and Horacio. Celestia was at a table in the corner with a dozen pieces of paper and a two-bit pencil in her hand as she worked on the company books.

"Howdy, Captain," Nick said with a smile that showed a row of white teeth. "How about a whiskey to wash the dust off your gullet?"

"Why, I don't mind if I do," Blade said. As he sipped, it was clear he had something on his mind he wanted to share. "I've come here to make a proposal."

Horacio put his glass down, frowned and said, "And what's that, Boris?"

"Since you gentlemen have come to Tortuga, we have managed to restore the island to all its past glory. It is once again a safe haven and is thriving as it did a century ago. So, I must say that I feel my job here is coming to an end."

His words shocked Nick and Horacio. The Texan nearly choked on his drink as he spat out a mouthful of whiskey.

"What on earth for?" Nick asked as he wiped his mouth with the back of his hand.

"To be honest, I'm ready to enjoy life some without tending to problems," Blade said. "And I've come here to inform you of my choice to replace me."

Horacio and Nick looked from Captain Blade to each other and back again. They realized he was serious, and they were curious.

Nick asked, "And who might that be, partner?"

"I believe, after observing the progress of the past

months, you two together would do a fine job of governing Tortuga. Then, I could once again have the opportunity to sail on my beloved sea again. I haven't set sail for over a decade now, and I long for the ocean. The island will be in good hands, and I can retire, at least partially. Of course, I will always be available for any needs you may have. But my time to enjoy life a little has come. You both have made me a wealthy man again, and I can go where I please."

Horacio almost teared up at the thought of Blade leaving. They had been through a lot together; his help had been immeasurable. Even Nick, who had been suspicious of the governor from the beginning, was disappointed he had decided to give up his job. They understood his yearning to return to sail with the trade winds once again. There was nothing better than hopping from island to island, enjoying all the different cultures and languages that populated the Caribbean and the Gulf of Mexico.

That evening, the three men sat at the bar and drank whiskey until the early hours. Captain Blade dazzled them with stories of his adventures as a young pirate. As he spoke, they could see the fire ignite in his eyes after all the years on land. When he talked of the Atlantic and Pacific Oceans, it was like he was speaking of a lost love.

Finally, when Blade had his fill and was all talked out; he departed, leaving the two old friends on their own. A rooster crowed outside as the first vestiges of light shone through the glass window. An offshore breeze swept through the saloon, ruffling Nick's hair. The smell of sea salt was strong in the air.

"I think we ought to have a hoedown for Captain Blade and his retirement," Nick said.

"What is a hoedown?" Horacio asked as he raised an eyebrow.

"It's kind of like a shindig but more like a hootenanny. I can see you're still confused because your face has gone all catawampus."

"We've been partners for a considerable amount of time now. But, I must admit, at times, I have difficulty understanding you," Horacio said gleefully.

"Maybe we should sail to Galveston and take a holiday ourselves," Nick said. "It'd be nice to visit home for a spell."

"I have no one left in London, so there is no reason for me to return there," Horacio said. "But I wouldn't mind seeing America, especially this Texas you talk about so much. Maybe you might want to find a port of entry where you are not a wanted man, though."

"Aw, by now, there be another hundred outlaws to track down. Killings are a dime a dozen in Texas. I doubt they even remember me. I never killed nobody or nothin' anyway. I just winged a marshal by accident."

When they walked out onto the front porch, the morning sun had just breached the edge of the world to their right, sending a rainbow across the sky. Slices of red rays slashed at the heavens. The early breeze dropped off, making the morning muggy. The smell of firewood was in the air and plumes of smoke seeped from chimneys. Dogs barked, and the chains of a wagon clanked. The town was waking up to a new day and a new adventure, and both men knew the sky was the limit. Wherever their desires sent them, they would go.

a look at:

Abandoned (Benjie Willow the Orphan1)

A massacre stole everything—the trail to El Paso might give him a reason to keep going...

Fourteen-year-old Benjie Willow should've died with the rest of his family. Hidden in a water well as Comanche raiders swept through his ranch on the Red River, he emerged into a world he no longer recognized—alone, grieving, and hunted.

When seasoned frontiersman Malvo Tanner and the quiet Choctaw warrior Chito-Oche spot smoke on the horizon, they don't expect to find a terrified boy as the only survivor. Taking Benjie in, they set off for El Paso, dragging him through lawless lands where danger rides faster than justice... and the past haunts every mile.

But the West isn't kind to orphans, and as Benjie struggles to find his place in this brutal new world, he'll have to learn what it means to survive...not just in body, but in spirit.

Will the trail harden him into something unrecognizable...or forge a future he never dared to imagine?

AVAILABLE NOW

about the author

Born in 1886 in Southern Ohio, Ash Lingam grew crops, raised cattle, and doted on the young boy. Ash's family was among the early settlers in pre-Revolutionary America. He has traced his lineage back to around 1746 when his ancestors immigrated from Europe to the aspiring American Colonies.

A retired marketing executive, Ash devotes his spare time to training police dogs and writing novels. He has found his niche in the Western, historical fiction, and adventure genres. With his vast vault of experience, he never runs out of sources for new stories. He has lived in eleven different countries and worked in a total of forty-six to date, Ash has written approximately 130 novels, short stories, and poems. More than one hundred of his eclectic titles help the American frontier come alive for his readers.

https://www.ashlingam.com/